ICKY RICKY 1

TOILET PAPER MUMMY

-RIBBIT!

Written & illustrated by

MICHAEL REX

A STEPPING STONE BOOK™

Random House 🏠 New York

To Bob, who some say is a slob,
but I know him as a friend.

Copyright © 2013 by Michael Rex

All rights reserved. Published in the United States by
Random House Children's Books, a division of Random House, Inc., New York.

Random House and the colophon are registered trademarks and
A Stepping Stone Book and the colophon are trademarks of Random House, Inc.

Visit us on the Web!
SteppingStonesBooks.com
randomhouse.com/kids

Educators and librarians, for a variety of teaching tools,
visit us at RHTeachersLibrarians.com

Library of Congress Cataloging-in-Publication Data
Rex, Michael.
Toilet paper mummy / written and illustrated by Michael Rex.
p.   cm. — (Icky Ricky ; #1)
"A Stepping Stone Book."
Summary: Icky Ricky finds his way into all sorts of messes, from having
a sleepover on the ceiling, to launching his pet hot dog into his father's
toolbox, to being shot with his favorite food, Cheese-in-a-Can.
ISBN 978-0-307-93167-2 (pbk.) — ISBN 978-0-375-97101-3 (lib. bdg.) —
ISBN 978-0-307-97538-6 (ebook)
[1. Behavior—Fiction. 2. Humorous stories.] I. Title.
PZ7.R32875Tnm 2013
[E]—dc23   2012025090

Printed in the United States of America

10 9 8 7 6 5 4 3 2 1

Random House Children's Books supports
the First Amendment and celebrates the right to read.

CONTENTS

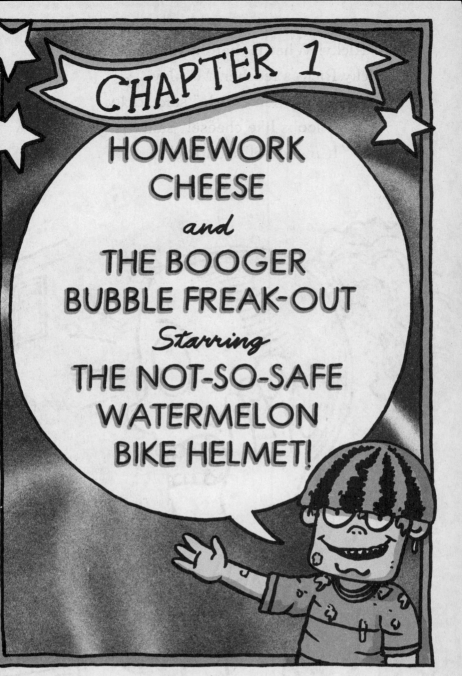

"Ricky! What is that on your face?" asked
Icky Ricky's teacher, Ms. Jay.

"It's my homework," said Ricky.

"It looks like cheese!" said Ms. Jay.

"It *is* cheese!" said Ricky.

"Why, oh why, Ricky, is your homework made out of cheese?" asked Ms. Jay.

"Because I couldn't find my bike helmet!" said Ricky.

"I don't understand," said Ms. Jay.

Yesterday, Gus came over to my house and wanted to go bike riding. I couldn't find my bike helmet. So instead of wasting time looking for it, I decided to make one.

I brought a watermelon from the kitchen out to the front steps. I cut it in half with a plastic knife because I'm not allowed to use real knives. That took forever. Then I scooped out all the insides. I put the watermelon on my head. It looked really cool. Then Gus wanted a watermelon helmet, too. So we made his from the other half of the watermelon.

We didn't know if the helmets were safe for bike riding, so we tested them. We dropped things on them, like a book, *splop!* And a shoe, *clomp!* And a wrench, *blonk!* And then a really big book, *kasplop!* Then we did one more test. We ran into a wall as hard as we could.

The helmets cracked, and the juices and gunk ran all over our faces. We couldn't go bike riding.

All that testing had made us hungry. We went back to the steps and scraped the watermelon insides into a bowl. But there were ants in the insides now, and a leaf and a stick. I don't eat ants. (It's not fair to them.) We let the ants have the watermelon, and we picked out the seeds.

WATERMELON SEEDS!

ANT!

We decided to have a seed-spitting contest. We spit our first seeds across the lawn but couldn't find them in the grass. Gus figured the seeds would be easier to find inside, so we went to my room. At first we weren't very good, and the seeds went all over the place. One went into the fishbowl, one went under my sheets, and one stuck to a lightbulb. We needed targets. I took all my homework papers from my folder and drew monsters and aliens and stuff on them. We spit and spit and spit.

DOINK

We got really good and could hit the
targets right between the eyes from all the
way out in the hallway. We were awesome.

We got tired of spitting seeds since we were experts now, so Gus did a trick for me. He turned his eyelids inside out so I could see the pink side. It was freaking me out.

I was like, "You're freaking me out!"

And Gus said, "Am I *totally* freaking you out?"

Then I told him, "Yes, you're *totally* freaking me out!"

Gus said, "How much am I freaking you out?"

And I was like, "You're freaking me out so much that . . . that . . . I have to blow a booger bubble!" So I blew the biggest booger bubble I could, and we cracked up all over the place.

Gus went home, and I had to do my homework. I'd used all my paper for the seed targets. (I looked for clean sheets of paper but I couldn't find any.) Then I started to think real hard. What else could I write on? What else is smooth and bright and flat? I thought the walls or my bedroom door would be good, but I couldn't get them to school in my backpack.

Then I figured out that cheese would work. First I tried to write on it with a pencil, but the pencil ripped it up. So I ate that slice. Then I tried a crayon, but that just smushed the cheese and didn't really show up. So I ate that slice. Then I tried a marker. That worked. It smeared a little, but if I blew on the cheese, it dried pretty well. The marker was like . . .

I did my homework and filled nine pieces
of cheese. I used the last slice of cheese to
make a sign that said "Ricky is Awesome!"
Then I stuck it to my wall. It stayed, even
without tape or glue. Then I went to bed.

I woke up late, and my mom was telling me to hurry. I went to put the homework in my backpack, but it was stuck to my desk. I tried to peel the cheese off my desk, but it just ripped. I used a flyswatter to scrape the slices off and stuck them in my folder. One got all rolled up, but I was able to fix it.

My mom was yelling, "C'mon, Ricky! You'll miss the bus! You'll be late for school!" So I had to leave without eating breakfast.

On the bus I was getting really, really hungry. I didn't want to eat my lunch, because then I wouldn't have lunch at lunchtime. So I started to eat the cheese, even though it was my homework. At first I couldn't even taste the marker, but after two slices it got kind of gross. Then Gus was like, "What are you eating?"

I told him I was eating homework cheese.

And then Stew was like "Hey, I love cheese. Can I try homework cheese?"

So Gus and Stew tried a slice of homework cheese. They didn't like it. We bit holes in the cheese and made bank robber masks. They stuck to our faces without any strings or anything.

Gus still had some watermelon seeds
in his pockets, so then we decorated the
masks and made them look even cooler.

"Don't they look cool, Ms. Jay?" Ricky asked.

"Yes, Ricky, they look cool," Ms. Jay said. "It seems like you really tried to do your homework. Do it tonight, and I will accept it."

"I don't know if I can do it tonight," said Ricky.

"Why not?" asked Ms. Jay.

"Because," said Ricky . . .

I'M ALL OUT OF CHEESE!

ICKY RICKY'S TIME-SAVING TIP #1

SNACKS!

Life can get really busy, and you need food to give you energy. I always have a snack on hand so I don't get slowed down.

Spaghetti is a great snack. It's easy to make, fun to eat, and fits into any size pocket! You can even ball it up and keep it in your sock or your hat.

THAT'S NOT HAIR!

If spaghetti seems dull for a snack, spice it up with a meatball and extra tomato sauce. Meatballs and sauce also fit well into most any pocket!

For the kid on the go, spaghetti is the answer!

And remember, kids, plastic is bad for the earth and harmful to the environment. Skip the plastic bags and stuff this yummy treat anywhere you can. You'll be ready for a fun-filled, high-energy, spaghetti-powered day!

Mean Dean was walking right toward Ricky. "Dude, why are you covered with yellow paint, and why do you have baloney and dog hair all over you?" he asked in his mean voice.

"That's a long story, Dean," said Ricky.

Dean's little sister, Samantha, came up behind Ricky.

"Why are you wearing that stupid hat, and where is my remote-controlled car?" Dean asked her angrily.

Samantha looked at Ricky. She was about to cry.

Ricky started to explain, "That's what I was going to tell you about, Dean. . . ."

Samantha came over to my house this morning, trying to sell her toys. She was like, "I drove my brother's remote-controlled car into Black Pond, and I need money to buy him a new one. Do you want to buy some of my toys?" But all she had were girls' toys, like Glitter Pony Superstar, Pinky Pink Pals, Poo-Poo Cutie Kittens, and Poo-Poo Cutie Kitten Babies. I didn't have any money anyway, so I asked her if she wanted me to try to get the RC car out of the pond for her, and she was like, "Yes! Yes!"

We went down to the pond, and she
showed me where the car drove off the
footbridge. We looked real hard from the
bridge, but the water in that pond is so
black and scummy that you can't see the
bottom. I walked around to the side of the
bridge and stepped into the pond.

I kept my shoes on, because I know
a lot of people throw junk and garbage
in the water. One time I saw a whole air
conditioner in there, and another time I
saw a kid throw in a notebook on the last
day of school.

I walked through the water to where Samantha was pointing, and I started to feel around. I pulled something out! It was an old baseball glove. I was like, "Cool! I'm keeping this." Then with my other hand, I pulled out an old can of soda, and it wasn't even opened. I stuffed it into my pocket to keep for later. I kept digging around and finding all these cool things, like an old windshield wiper, a deflated soccer ball, a CD, and a baseball hat. But I couldn't find the car. I put my head underwater to look for it, but the water was too dirty.

Something tickled my leg. I reached in and pulled out a frog. I asked Sam if she wanted to give the frog to you, but she said you would still want your RC car. I closed my eyes, bent down, and felt around one more time. I grabbed something, stood up, and yanked. Whatever it was, it was really stuck. I pulled and pulled, but it wouldn't move. I needed both hands but I didn't want to lose the frog, and Samantha wouldn't hold it, so I put it in my mouth. I didn't bite it or anything, I just held it with my lips. I put both hands on the thing I was pulling and tugged really hard.

It yanked free and shot into the air.
It was underwear! Huge underwear! Huge,
old, pond-scum underwear! It flew into
the sky and blocked the sun! It was an
underwear eclipse! The frog freaked and
jumped out of my mouth and landed on
Samantha's head. She started screaming
like crazy! Then the underwear landed on
my head, like, *splat!*

OOOSH!

Dean interrupted Ricky. "Dude, this story is stupid. What's it got to do with my remote-controlled car?"

"Just wait," said Ricky, "there's more!"

TO BE CONTINUED . . .

"Ricky!" his mom cried as she walked into his bedroom. "Why are you guys sleeping on the ceiling?"

"Because we ate too much junk food!" said Ricky.

"That makes no sense," said his mom.

"Sure it does," said Ricky. "Let me explain. . . ."

Last night, when Gus and Stew came over for our sleepover, the first thing we did was get out all the food we had. We had chips, pickles, candy bars, peanut butter, ketchup, juice, popcorn, pizza, and Cheese-in-a-Can. This was a great way to start a sleepover.

We started watching monster movies. First we saw a vampire movie. We put ketchup in our mouths, and when the vampires bit people, we let it dribble out.

A monster movie came on about a big spider that spun giant webs and trapped all these people. It was pretty lame, so we decided it would be better in 3-D. I hid behind the TV while Gus and Stew watched. Every time the spider made his web, I shot the Cheese-in-a-Can at Gus and Stew. It was great, and it made the movie awesome. At first Gus and Stew dodged the spray, but then they tried to see if they could catch it in their mouths.

That movie ended and a space movie came on. We made that 3-D, too. Every time someone shot a laser, I sprayed the cheese again. There were asteroids in this movie. We used popcorn to make that part 3-D. We chucked it all over the place when the asteroids were shooting through space. We noticed that the popcorn stuck anywhere there was Cheese-in-a-Can cheese, even to our shirts.

Then we started throwing popcorn at each other, and the person with the most popcorn on his shirt was the loser, so we tried to eat the popcorn when no one was looking.

But we didn't have any more Cheese-in-a-Can, so we covered our shirts with peanut butter and tossed more popcorn at each other. It was awesome.

We ran out of popcorn, so we decided
to see if the pickles would stick to our
shirts. I chucked one at Stew and *plop,*
it fell on the floor. They were too heavy,
so we ate a few and had Pickle Olympics.
We did the pickle toss, pickle soccer,
pickle hacky sack, and then freestyle pickle
gymnastics.

That was the easiest. All you had to
do was move your body all crazy and stuff
while holding a pickle in your mouth.

We kept eating the chips and the candy bars and any popcorn we could find. The peanut-butter-covered popcorn was better than the Cheese-in-a-Can-covered popcorn. But we all started feeling like we were going to barf. We had eaten too much junk food. I really felt like barf was coming up my throat. Stew said my brain wouldn't let me barf on my favorite toy, so he held it in front of my face. And you know what? I didn't barf! It was like magic. We needed to feel better, so I said we should eat something healthy, like soup.

We snuck down to the kitchen to make
soup. None of us had ever made soup, so we
just started grabbing things that might be in
soup and put them all in a bowl. We found an
onion, a carrot, some beans, some broccoli,
and a mango. We looked for a potato but
couldn't find one, so we used frozen French
fries. Soup should have some meat, so we put
in a fish stick.

I found my bike helmet in the freezer.
I put it back in there so I could stay cool
the next time I went biking.

We tried stirring all the soup stuff in
the bowl, but it wasn't getting soupy. Gus
said we should mash it up, so we put it in
a plastic bag and whacked it with spoons.

We were making too much noise, so we
went back to my room. We kept trying to
mash the stuff up, but it still wasn't soupy.
We poured in the leftover pickle juice to
make it soupier. We put the bag between
some books and smushed it. We put it
under my mattress and rolled on it. Finally,
Stew stood on it and that worked a little.
Then I had my best idea of the night.

I put the bag on the floor and climbed
up on my dresser. I jumped as high as
I could and came down hard on the soup
bag. It exploded! The soup gunk shot all
over Gus, all over Stew, and all over the
wall and the floor. It was awesome!

We tasted the soup, but it wasn't very good. We were all pretty tired by now, so we got out our sleeping bags, but the floor was so totally covered with soup gunk and popcorn and pickles and ketchup and cheese that there was nowhere to put them. I was trying to think where else we could sleep. Maybe in the basement? Maybe outside? Maybe in the attic? Then I had the perfect idea.

WHAT ABOUT THE CEILING?

We covered our sleeping bags with lots of peanut butter, tons of ketchup, and anything else sticky we could find. We tossed the sleeping bags up to the ceiling, and they stuck. Then we climbed onto my desk, across my dresser, and into the bags.

Right before we fell asleep, we started to make a list of all the foods that should come in a can, like Tacos-in-a-Can and Pizza-in-a-Can and Pickles-in-a-Can and Toast-in-a-Can and Homework-Cheese-in-a-Can. And then we fell asleep. That's why we are sleeping on the ceiling.

"Oh . . . okay," said Mom. "Come on down, and I'll make some breakfast."

"That's okay," said Ricky. "We thought of that last night and stuck the pizza to the ceiling, too."

CLEANING YOUR ROOM!

Cleaning your room is a big drag and eats up valuable kid time. That's why I keep my room organized alphabetically.

"**A**" items, such as airplane parts, art supplies, and antique sandwiches, go "**A**ll over."

"**B**" items, such as baseball gloves, balloons, and baboon costumes, go "**B**eneath everything else."

KEEP A LIST SO YOU KNOW WHERE THINGS ARE.

"**C**" items, such as clothes, cookies, and collectibles, get stuffed in the "**C**loset."

And "**D**" items, such as dinosaur toys, dishes, and dirty socks, are "**D**umped in drawers."

Get it? Let this handy-dandy tip keep you organized so you have time to play with your friends, explore the bottom of a pond, and send pizza to your pen pal in Japan!

CHAPTER 4

MEAN DEAN'S
REMOTE-CONTROLLED
CAR (PART 2)

Featuring

THE LEMONADE MAN,
BALONEY STRAWS,

and

THE HAIRY, SLOBBERY
BALONEY-SNATCHING
DOG!

Mean Dean was staring at Samantha and Ricky. "I still don't know why you are covered with all that yellow paint, and I still don't have my car."

"Well, just listen," said Ricky. . . .

We gave up trying to find the car in the pond, and Samantha was about to cry, so I said I would help her get money for a new one. We realized that selling toys wouldn't work, because only kids want toys, but kids don't have money. We needed something adults would buy. Then I had a great idea! "Why don't we set up a lemonade stand?" I said, and Samantha said, "Yes," and we ran back to my house.

We found one little packet of lemonade
mix in the kitchen. We mixed it up fast,
but didn't read the directions and put in too
much water. It didn't taste lemony enough,
so we searched around and found some
lemon cough drops and put them in. They
looked like little lemon ice cubes. It tasted
better, but not quite right, so we stirred
in some sugar. Now it was too thick, and I
was like, "Man, making lemonade is hard,"
and then I had my best idea of the day. The
soda I found in the pond was lemon-lime!
I poured it in. It tasted awesome!

We ran to the garage and found some yellow paint. Samantha made signs and I set up a little table. It looked excellent, but no one bought any lemonade. We were screaming our guts out, like, "Lemonade, lemonade, get your ice-cold lemonade!" But still no one bought any.

I held one of the signs up high for people to see, and I got some yellow paint on me and that gave me an idea. I grabbed the paint from the garage and started painting all over my face, my arms, my

shirt, and my pants. Then I found an old
football helmet and painted that yellow, too.
Samantha painted a little kid cowboy hat
to wear. I was like, "I'll be the Lemonade
Man!" I looked really cool, and then I started
dancing around on the sidewalk and shaking
my butt and stuff and singing,

We still sold nothing. Samantha said we had to have a gimmick to sell the lemonade, and I asked, "Like what?" She said maybe we could give away a free straw with each cup. I thought that was a great idea. I ran to the kitchen and looked around. No straws. I was thinking that maybe I could make straws. I needed something thin that I could roll up. Baloney! Yes!

① ← SLICE OF BALONEY
② ROLLED UP
③ BALONEY STRAW!

THREE CHEERS FOR BALONEY!

I ran back to the table with some baloney and showed Samantha how to make a baloney straw. We made a bunch and put them in the cups. We had a few extra slices so I stuck them on my shirt like polka dots. Again, we sold nothing!

Then I had my second-best idea of the day! "We should sell door to door!" I said, and we grabbed some cups and straws and started ringing people's doorbells. Everyone was like, "No, thank you," and then they closed the door in my face before I even did my Lemonade Man dance.

Finally, the man at the end of the
street said "Yes" to the lemonade, but
he didn't want a baloney straw. He was
getting his money when all of a sudden his
big dog came running to the door, jumped
up, and snatched the baloney polka dots.
I got knocked down off the stoop, and the
lemonade and baloney straws spilled all
over me! I was lucky I had my helmet on.

WOOOF!

The dog jumped on top of me and
started gobbling up the baloney, and his
dog hair was sticking to the paint, and his
slobber was flying all over the place!

"Ricky!" screamed Dean.

TO BE CONTINUED . . .

"Ricky!" shouted Ricky's dad as he came around the corner of the house and saw Ricky, Gus, and Stew. "Why did a hot dog with a mustache fall out of the sky and into my toolbox?"

"Because it was his birthday wish!" said Ricky.

"Whose birthday wish?" asked Dad.

"Harry's," said Ricky.

"Who is Harry?" asked Ricky's dad.

"He's my pet hot dog, and I'm glad you found him!" said Ricky.

"Ricky," said his dad quietly, "start from the beginning."

"All right . . ."

I woke up today and realized it was Harry's birthday. I looked all over for him, and then I remembered that I left him in the hamper ("H" for "Hamper," "H" for "Harry"), so I dug around and there he was, under a dirty dish I used for eating a hamburger. It had been so long since I had seen him that he had grown hair!

BEFORE!

The first thing I needed to do for his birthday was give him a haircut. I used Mom's fancy little makeup scissors to snip away most of the fuzz.

Part of the hair I couldn't cut away. It looked like a funky beard. But if you have a funky beard, you need a funky mustache. I reached between my toes and picked some fuzz, then I stuck my finger in my ear to get some earwax. I used the earwax to stick the toe fuzz to his face, like an awesome mustache. Then I redrew his eyes. He looked ready to party.

Once that was done, I had to figure out what to get Harry for his birthday. I looked around the house for ideas. I've lost Harry a few times. Once I lost him in my backpack, once he fell behind the toilet, and once I left him outside overnight. *That's it*, I thought. *I'll build him his own house so I can't ever lose him again.*

I grabbed some old shoe boxes, some scissors, some paints, and some glitter. I cut the box and made a house with two rooms. Then I painted the walls and poured glitter on them. But I didn't have any glue. How was I going to stick all this together?

I thought, *Mayonnaise looks like glue! I'll use that.* I got some mayonnaise from the fridge and brushed it all over the hot dog house. It began to fall apart. I needed to find something stickier. Maple syrup! I grabbed some from the kitchen and squirted it all over the house. The syrup held Harry's house together, and it was looking pretty cool.

The house needed a TV. Somewhere
in my room I had a little TV-shaped pencil
sharpener. I crawled under my bed and
shoved some junk around. Finally, I found
it. I also found a cookie that I lost in the

first grade. The bad thing was, I was
covered with syrup and mayonnaise and
paint, and the dust fuzz from under my bed
was stuck all over me.

I sneezed over and over. I tried to cover
my mouth, but my hand was all painty and
covered with syrup. Dust fuzz is the one thing
I don't like because it makes me sneezy and
makes my nose drip boogers like crazy. Now I
would have to take a bath before the party.

I was thinking that I would invite Gus and Stew to the party. I could make really fancy invitations with the glitter and stuff. But that was a waste of time. I opened the window and just shouted,

I only had an hour and a whole ton of
stuff to do. I had to wash my clothes, take
a bath, make sandwiches, and bake a cake.
I didn't know if I could do it all, but then
I saw my cheese sign that said "Ricky is
Awesome!" and I knew I could do it!

When you think about it, it doesn't
make any sense to wash your clothes in
one place, and wash your body in another
place, and make lunch in another place.

Right? So I decided to do them all at once.
I grabbed the peanut butter and the jelly
and a few slices of bread and potato chips,
cookies, and some jelly beans. I brought
them into the bathroom. I filled up the tub.
Then I jumped in with my clothes on and
laid out the food on the side of the tub.

I didn't have enough bowls and plates, so
I had the great idea of putting everything in
a sandwich. Since I forgot to bring a knife
to spread the peanut butter and jelly, I used
a toy hammerhead shark that I keep in the
bathtub. I was kind of splashing around and
the bread was getting wet when I knocked
the chips into the tub.

I scooped up the chips. I got some of the dust fuzz that was floating around in the water, too, but I didn't think anyone would notice. I crumbled the cookies on

top of the peanut butter and jelly, put the jelly beans on, and put on another slice of bread. The sandwiches looked awesome.

A slice of bread fell in the tub and
floated around. I stood up, aimed my shark,
and dropped my shark on it.

It tore a perfect hole right through
the bread. I splashed around some more in
the water to make sure I was clean, and
I stepped out of the tub.

By accident, I knocked the sandwiches onto the floor. Those sandwiches were sure taking a beating! I picked them up and tried to dry them with the toilet paper. It just stuck to them. And to me. Actually it was kind of cool. I stuck some toilet paper to my belly and started spinning around and around. Soon I looked like a mummy. What an awesome way to look for a birthday party. Then I was like,

OH NO! I FORGOT TO MAKE A CAKE!

I ran to the kitchen. I found a box of cake mix and some icing. The directions on the box said the cake takes forty-five minutes to cook! Forty-five minutes? Yeah, right! I only had five. I had to think fast. I poured the cake-mix powder into a big bowl. Then I scooped the icing into the bowl. I mushed it all up with my hands and made it into a tube shape. It didn't really look like a cake. It looked like a log. So I called it the cake-log-thing. I tried to write "Happy Birthday" on it with mustard, but I ran out of room. It only said "Happy Birt."

CAKE-LOG-THING

Gus and Stew came over, and they
wanted to be toilet paper mummies, too.
They ran to the bathroom, jumped in the
tub, got soaked, and then got all rolled up.
We started jumping around and playing air
guitar, mummy-style.

This was turning into the best party
ever. We tried to eat the sandwiches, but
they had gotten too soggy and toilet-papery
and fell apart. The jelly beans were still
good so we picked those out and ate them.
We ran around the house as mummies for
a while, but then we got thinking about
candy and hitting things and wanted to do
the piñata. Every party has a piñata!

We needed to make a piñata. I looked
around the house for something strong
enough to hold stuff but that would break
with a stick. I took one of Mom's garbage
bags. The box says that they are strong
and tough, but Mom rolls her eyes and says
they're cheapo and always rip.

We ran to the kitchen to fill the bag with candy. First we dropped in the few jelly beans that were left, but that hardly filled the bag. We needed something else. We added the leftover cookies.

The bag still wasn't full. Gus had some watermelon seeds in his pocket so he put them in. We opened the fridge. What else could go in the piñata?

Gus was like, "Salami?"

And I was like, "No."

Stew was like, "Frozen waffles?"

And I was like, "No."

Then Gus was like, "Celery?"

And I was like, "No."

And then Stew was like, "Eggs?"

And I was like,

EGGS? EGGS! YEAH, EGGS!

We love eggs! Gus loves fried eggs. Stew loves scrambled eggs. I love poached eggs.

We decided the eggs looked kind of boring and white, so we drew faces and stuff on them with markers. Only three broke, which we thought was pretty good.

Then we put them in the bag and tied the top. We drew a big face on the bag to make it look more like a piñata. Then I put an old baseball hat on it and some broken sunglasses. He was looking awesome.

Gus held him up and said, "It's Señor Piñata Dude!"

And then Stew said, *"¡Buenos dias, Señor!"*

And I said, *"¿Dondé esta el Queso-en-una-Lata?"* which means "Where is the Cheese-in-a-Can?" I think.

Then I found some string and tied it to the top of the bag, and we were done. We ran outside and tied one end of the string to a branch, and then we each grabbed a stick.

We were gonna take turns and be all polite and stuff, but we were having so much fun that we all started swinging and smacking Señor Piñata Dude like crazy. The cheap bag exploded, and the eggs shot out, and the jelly beans flew in the air, and the cookie crumbs and watermelon seeds stuck all over us. We laughed so hard that we rolled in the yard, and the eggy goop picked up leaves and sticks and dirt.

But you know what? I was a horrible
party thrower. We never gave Harry his
cake, and he never even got a shot at his
piñata. So I went inside and got him and
the cake-log-thing. We sang "Happy Birt"
to Harry, and we ate the cake-log-thing.
It wasn't that bad, unless you bit into a big
chunk of powder mix. Then I asked Harry
what his birthday wish was. Stew and Gus
were like, "Dude, hot dogs can't talk."

101

And I was like,

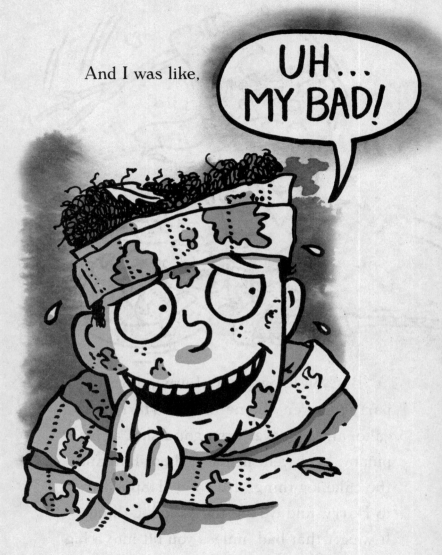

UH... MY BAD!

Then we were cracking up again, and we decided that since all of us wished we could fly, then Harry must want to fly, too!

We tied him to the piñata
string and started swinging
him around and around and
around. It's really hard to tie
a string to a hot dog, and he
slipped out of the knot and
shot off over the house.

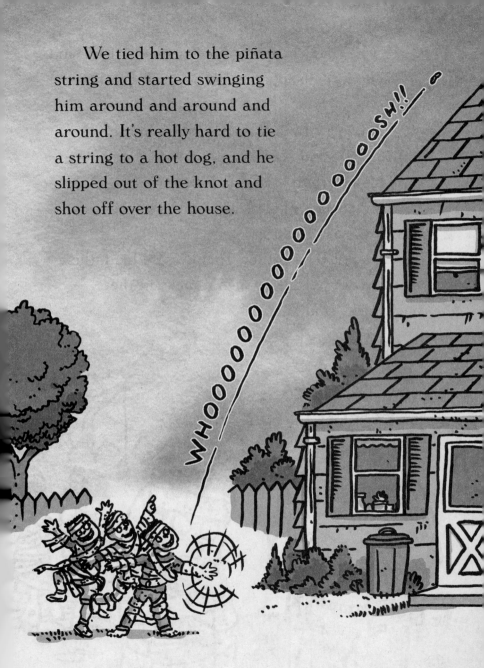

WHOOOOOOOOOOOOOOOOOOOSH!!

"See, Dad? It makes total sense," Ricky said.

"I'm very disappointed, Ricky," his father said.

"I'm sorry I made such a mess in the bathroom," said Ricky.

"It's not that," said his father.

"I'm sorry I made such a mess in the kitchen," said Ricky.

"It's not that, either, Ricky," said his father.

"I'm sorry I made such a mess in the backyard," said Ricky.

"It's not that, either, Ricky," said his
father. "I'm disappointed that you threw
this wonderful party for Harry, and you
didn't even invite Pete."

105

ICKY RICKY'S TIME-SAVING TIP #3

BRUSHING YOUR TEETH!

Kids need to brush their teeth, but we don't always have the time. Kids are busy people. Between school, homework, and playing, who has time to brush three times a day?

I BARELY HAVE TIME TO CHANGE MY UNDERWEAR!

That's why I put a little toothpaste into every meal. I mix a tiny bit in with my cereal in the morning. Just a smidge works as a tasty sandwich spread at lunch, and a pea-sized glob as a treat at dinner!

When I'm done with my meal, my teeth
are clean, and my breath is fresh!

Not only that, but I'm not wasting
water by brushing. And I'm not polluting
the environment by throwing away old
toothbrushes!

It leaves me lots of time to work on my
new cookbook, too:

*101 Awesome Dishes to Make with Cheese-
in-a-Can!*

#37, CHEESE-IN-A-CAN PANCAKES!

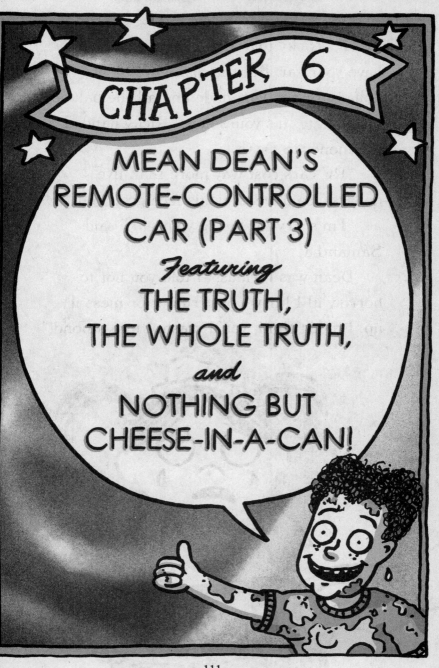

"Well," Ricky told Mean Dean, "we don't have your car. But the man gave us five dollars for the lemonade and all the baloney his dog ate. It's yours now." Ricky handed the money to Dean.

"RC cars cost way more than five dollars!" said Dean as his face grew red.

"I'm sorry for losing your car," said Samantha.

Dean was furious! "I told you not to borrow it! I knew you'd ruin it or mess it up. I didn't think you'd crash it into a pond!"

"I said I'm sorry. I didn't mean to lose it," said Samantha, and she started to cry.

"I don't care!" Dean yelled. "You know what I'm going to do? I'm going to go up to your room, get your dolls, and throw them in Black Pond."

"What?" cried Samantha.

"If I can't have my car, you can't have your dolls! Mr. Monkey and Mr. Donkey are going in the pond!" He turned to go back to his house.

"No! No! No! I'm sorry! You can't!"
Samantha grabbed his shirt and tried to
stop him.

"I'm doing it!" shouted Dean.

"Wait!" Ricky broke in.

I DID IT! I LOST YOUR RC CAR!

Dean looked back. "Huh?"

"I was driving it when it went in the
pond . . . not Samantha," said Ricky.

Samantha looked at Ricky. He talked so fast she couldn't get a word in.

"It's my fault," said Ricky. "What are you going to do about it?"

"I can't believe you made my sister lie to me!" said Dean. "She's just a little kid, jerk!" He hugged Samantha. "Don't worry, Samantha, I won't chuck out your dolls." He looked at Ricky. "You're a real creep, Ricky!"

Ricky put on his best guilty face. "Yeah, well, I'm a creep," he said. "I'm the creep who lost your RC car, and I'm the creep covered with dog slobber and yellow paint. I don't know what you're going to do to me, Dean. I really don't. I don't know if you're going to beat me up, throw my stuff in Black Pond, or say mean things about me in school. I just don't know."

Ricky got down on his knees.

JUST PLEASE, PLEASE, PLEASE DO NOT SPRAY ME WITH CHEESE-IN-A-CAN! I CAN'T STAND THAT STUFF! IT'S THE MOST DISGUSTING, HORRIBLE, NASTIEST STUFF IN THE WHOLE WORLD! I GAG WHEN I SMELL IT! I GET A RASH WHEN I TOUCH IT! JUST LOOKING AT IT MAKES ME WANT TO

"Dude, you shouldn't have said that!"
said Dean as he ran back to his house.

"Thanks," said Samantha. She smiled
a great big smile at Ricky.

Dean ran back from the house with a
can of Cheese-in-a-Can!

"Oh no! Not Cheese-in-a-Can!" shouted
Ricky. He covered his head. Dean started
spraying the stuff all over him.

"Stop! Stop! I can't stand it!" cried Ricky.
"I'm gagging! I'm gagging! I'm getting sick!
My skin is burning! Stop! Stop!" He rolled
on the ground, and Dean kept showering
him with the cheese. Ricky turned his head
from Dean and looked at Samantha. Dean
couldn't see Ricky laughing!

121

101 AWESOME DISHES TO MAKE WITH CHEESE-IN-A-CAN! FEATURING...

Cheese-in-a-Can Sandwich

Cheese-in-a-Can Stew

Cheese-in-a-Can Sushi

Grilled Cheese-in-a-Can

Cheese-in-a-Can Cupcakes (the Cheese-in-a-Can is inside!)

and

Cheese-in-a-Can-Covered Honey-Mustard, Chocolate-Syrup Hot Wings!

DON'T MISS THE NEXT EXCITING ICKY RICKY BOOK!

ICKY RICKY 2

THE END OF THE WORLD

ALVIN HO

ALLERGIC TO GIRLS, SCHOOL, AND OTHER SCARY THINGS

BY Lenore LOOK   PICTURES BY LeUyen Pham

A Yearling Book

This is a work of fiction. Names, characters, places, and incidents either are the product of the author's imagination or are used fictitiously. Any resemblance to actual persons, living or dead, events, or locales is entirely coincidental.

Text copyright © 2008 by Lenore Look
Illustrations copyright © 2008 by LeUyen Pham

All rights reserved. Published in the United States by Yearling, an imprint of Random House Children's Books, a division of Random House, Inc., New York. Originally published in hardcover by Schwartz & Wade Books, an imprint of Random House Children's Books, in 2008.

Yearling and the jumping horse design are registered trademarks of Random House, Inc.

Visit us on the Web! www.randomhouse.com/kids

Educators and librarians, for a variety of teaching tools, visit us at
www.randomhouse.com/teachers

The Library of Congress has cataloged the hardcover edition of this work as follows:

Look, Lenore.
Alvin Ho allergic to girls, school, and other scary things / [text by] Lenore Look ; illustrated by LeUyen Pham.
p. cm.
Summary: A young boy in Concord, Massachusetts, who loves superheroes and comes from a long line of brave Chinese farmer-warriors, wants to make friends, but first he must overcome his fear of everything.
ISBN: 978-0-375-83914-6 (hardcover) — ISBN: 978-0-375-93914-3 (lib. bdg.) — ISBN: 978-0-375-84965-7 (e-book)
[1. Fear—Fiction. 2. Self-confidence—Fiction. 3. Friendship—Fiction. 4. Chinese Americans—Fiction.
5. Concord (Mass.)—Fiction.] I. Pham, LeUyen, ill. II. Title.
PZ7.L8682Al 2008
[Fic]—dc22
2007029456

ISBN: 978-0-375-84930-5 (pbk.)

Printed in the United States of America

10 9 8 7 6 5 4 3 2 1

First Yearling Edition

Random House Children's Books supports the First Amendment and celebrates the right to read.

Once Upon a Time

the first thing you should know about me is that my name is Alvin Ho.

I am afraid of many things.

Elevators.

Tunnels.

Bridges.

Airplanes.

Thunder.

Substitute teachers.

Kimchi.

Wasabi.

The dark.

Heights.

Scary movies.

Scary dreams.

Shots.

School.

If there were no school, my troubles would blast away, just like that. I would dig holes all day. I would play catch with my gunggung. I would watch cooking shows. I would keep an eye on things. It would be fantastic!

The second thing you should know about me is that even though I am afraid of many things, I am not afraid of anything that explodes. I love explosions. I was practically born with gunpowder in my blood! This is on account of I live in Concord, Massachusetts, which is hard to spell, but where there were explosions all over the place, when the American Revolutionary War started way before I was born.

The third thing you should know about me is

that I have a dog named Lucy and a brother named Calvin and a sister named Anibelly, who messes with my sticks and toys, eats my food, drinks my chocolate milk and gets in my way.

I am not as big as Calvin, but I am bigger than Anibelly, who isn't a baby anymore but doesn't go to school yet. I am sort of nearly almost medium . . . when I stand on tiptoe and stretch at the same time, I am finally almost visible in my class picture!

The fourth thing you should know about me is that I love Plastic Man, Wonder Woman, the Green Lantern, Concrete Man, Aquaman, King

Henry V and all the superheroes in the world. I know them from reading with my dad every night while my mom runs on the treadmill like a hamster on a wheel. My dad is a great reader for his age, which could be fifty or one hundred, it's hard to tell. He wears reading glasses and always puts one arm around me and his other arm around Anibelly and Calvin for support, on account of when you get to be that old, it is hard to do anything by yourself.

The fifth thing you should know about me is that once upon a time, before I went to school, I was a superhero. I was Firecracker Man! I ran around our house, full speed ahead, screaming at the top of my lungs while beating on a garbage can lid. I was as noisy as a firecracker on Chinese New Year! My costume was great (my gunggung made it).

But now I am Firecracker Man only on weekends and holidays. There's just no time for it.

Being a superhero is hard work. You have to save the world. But going to school is even harder. You have to save yourself. Most days I can hardly even make it to the school bus. And when I arrive at school, I can't think. I can't read. I can't smile. I can't sing. I can't scream.

I can't even talk.

The sixth thing you should know about me is that I have never spoken a word in school. Even when I try with all my might, I always manage to say nothing at all. My voice works at home. It works in the car. It even works on the school bus. But as soon as I get to school . . . I am as silent as a side of beef.

"You're like a piece of frozen sausage fallen off the truck," my brother, Calvin, likes to say. It is true. I am something like that.

No one really knows why I lose my voice at school, since I come from a long line of farmer-warriors who haven't had a scaredy bone in their

bodies since 714 AD. In China my ancient grandpas and grandmas and aunts and uncles fought off leopards and tigers in their gardens the way Calvin and Anibelly and I fight off mosquitoes at Walden Pond. They weren't afraid of anything. I am afraid of everything.

Getting — Gulp — Ready for School

it was the last day of summer vacation and Calvin and I were in our room getting ready for the first day of school. He was going into the fourth grade and I was heading into second. Calvin was on the computer and I was sitting on my bed going over my PDK—Personal Disaster Kit.

When you're afraid of everything, it's very important to carry a PDK. It's like a PFD, a Personal Flotation Device, only heavier and with more parts. A PDK begins with the right box. It must not be too big, like a shoe box, or too small,

like a Band-Aid tin. A handle
on it is good, but a lock is
bad on account of it will
keep you out when you
need to get in. I use a
waterproof fly box
with compart-
ments, which is
just perfect.

You can put anything in a PDK, but mostly it
should be things that are useful in a disaster, such as:

A whistle. If I lose my voice, a whistle is very
handy.

A three-leaf clover (because I couldn't find a
four-leaf one).

Garlic. For fending off vampires and teachers.

Dental floss. Handy for trapping, wrapping,
tying and hanging things (out of Anibelly's
reach).

Band-Aids.

 A magnifying glass. For general curiosity, but can also be used to start a fire.

 A mirror. For sending signals, in case you can't start a fire.

 A bandana. For preventing smoke inhalation, in case you start the above fire, but can also be used as a sling or a tourniquet.

 A scary mask. For keeping girls away.

 Escape routes.

The problem with PDKs, as everyone knows, is that they need to be updated every year on account of you never know what you'll need in the next grade. Now that I could read and write without help, I was adding something I'd needed for a long time—emergency plans.

I read them aloud to Calvin:

How to survive a fire in the school cafeteria.

1. Lie down. The freshest air is near the floor.

2. Crawl away from the flames.

3. RUN.

And...

How to meet your new teacher →

1. Put on a scary mask.

2. Rub on garlic.

3. Stay back 100 feet.

And...

> HOW TO SURVIVE SHOW-
> AND-
> TELL
>
> 1. Show something
>   Spectacular.
> 2. Hold it high.
> 3. Turn it around.
> 4. Listen to the
>   OO HS and AHHS.
>
> 5. Take a bow.

When I finished reading, I was very impressed with my plans.

But Calvin was not. "That's stupid," he said. Calvin is not supposed to use the s-word, it is bad.

"You can't say that," I said.

"Okay, it's *dumb*," said Calvin. "You're supposed to look your teacher in the eye, shake her hand and smile."

"But that's harder than putting on a scary mask," I said.

I am not too good at anything ever since I

started school, but Calvin is good at everything. He knows his multiplication tables, mostly. He has fantastic ideas for science projects. Most days he can finish his homework without falling asleep. And someday he will know something about everything because he is reading the entire encyclopedia online.

"Calvin," I said. "You're going to be the smartest person in the world."

"That's the whole idea," said Calvin, still reading. He needed to read pretty fast to give himself a jump-start on the fourth grade, which is when you have to speed-read to get yourself ready for middle school. He was up to the letter "D."

"Did you know that deer sleep only five minutes a day?" Calvin said.

"No," I said. "Calvin . . ."

Calvin ignored me and continued reading.

"The elephant is the only mammal that can't jump," he said.

Calvin was right. I've seen an elephant fly in a movie, but I've never seen one jump. "I need your help to finish my PDK," I said.

"I've already helped you," Calvin sighed. He did not look up.

"I need more help," I said. "I need emergency plans for making friends. None of the boys at school will play with me."

"That's because you're weird," said Calvin.

"I'm not weird," I said. "I have so-so performance anxiety disorder." It is true. I see a therapist for it.

"That's weird," said Calvin. He skipped ahead to "S."

"*You're* weird," I said.

"Did you know that the author William Shakespeare invented more than seventeen hundred words, including 'assassination' and 'bump'?"

I shook my head.

" 'Stewardesses' is the longest word you can type with only the left hand," said Calvin.

I growled.

Calvin stopped. "Okay," he said. "The first step in making friends is, don't talk so much. You need to be quiet. That is the first rule of being a good friend."

"Oh." I blinked. "But I can't talk in school!" I cried. "That's the problem!"

Calvin glared at me. "Maybe if you didn't use up all your words at home, you'd have some to use at school," he said.

I glared back.

"Okay," he said. "If I tell you, will you stop bothering me?"

"Okay," I agreed.

"Ready?" asked Calvin. "You better write fast."

So I did.

I read it twice.

Then I read it again.

CALVIN'S RULES for
Making FRiENDS
1. Say HELLO.
2. JUST say heLLo.
3. TRAde baseboll cards.
4. Trade MORE BaseBall CARds.
5. JUST trade Baseboll CARds.

It wasn't perfect, but I put it into my PDK and stopped bothering Calvin.

Roast Duck in the Window

after a while, I just had to bother Calvin again. He had stopped reading the encyclopedia online and was now sitting on the floor and holding a permanent marker in his hand.

"Whatcha doing?" I asked.

"I'm writing my name on everything I own," said Calvin. "That way, you'll have to ask for permission before you touch my stuff."

"Oh."

He wrote "Calvin Ho" on the

bottom of his sneakers. Then he wrote "C. Ho" in glistening black marker on the bottom of his baseball glove. "Calvin Ho" went inside his batting helmet. Finally, he began writing "Calvin Ho" inside his favorite books, which were also my favorite books.

It looked like I had better get started before everything belonged to Calvin!

So I grabbed another marker and wrote "Alvin Ho" on my baseball. It was not my play ball, but my special ball, kept in a clear plastic box on the shelf. Someone else had already written his name on it—Daisuke Matsuzaka, whose nickname is Dice-K. I can roll as fast as dice too, especially when I am Firecracker Man, so my name sure looked fantastic right next to his.

"Now that ball's good for nothing but playin'," said Calvin.

It was great news to me. I had always wanted to throw it.

But even better, Calvin seemed like he was now in a talking mood. So I gave him the bad news. "Calvin's Rules for Making Friends isn't going to work for me," I said. "I can't do anything on the list on account of I can't even say hello. Got any other ideas?"

"Hmmm," said Calvin, his marker in midair. "Are the other boys in your class bigger than you?"

"Mostly," I said, "but Pinky is bigger than everyone."

"Sometimes it helps if a friend is the same size as you," said Calvin. "Then you don't have to say anything."

"How come?" I asked.

"Dunno," said Calvin. "That's just the way it works."

Then Calvin went over to the computer, typed and clicked. "Stretching Exercises for Accelerated Growth" flashed across the screen. "See Results in Five Minutes! Amazing Results FAST!" There were all sorts of diagrams and instructions on how to grow a few inches. It was

perfect! He printed a few pages, and we hurried outside to the backyard with them.

Summer wasn't quite over, but fall was already showing off with pretty leaves. Butter-, cinnamon-, orange- and burnt-toast-colored, the leaves looked like fireworks exploding in the golden afternoon light. And Anibelly was singing under them.

"Lalalalalalala," Anibelly sang. "Lalalalalala."

Anibelly was digging holes, one of our favorite things to do. Her holes were not as good as mine—they weren't even real holes, just dimples— but she sure loved digging them.

"Lalalalalalala," she sang like a little bird. The garden hose was in one hand and one of my carved sticks was in the other.

I ran over. I nearly almost gave her a thumping, but I didn't. I remembered just in the nick of time that I am a gentleman. My dad taught me and Calvin the rules of being gentlemen. Rule

No. 1: No hitting, especially girls, unfortunately. If I remember only one rule it should be this, my dad said, and if I forget it, I will not be a man but a mushroom. Being a man would be a lot easier if Anibelly didn't mess with my things, eat my food, drink my chocolate milk or get in my way.

"Anibelly," I said, breathless. "That stick's been carved and it's not for digging, it's only for robbery and mayhem."

"Yup," said Anibelly. She stopped. She looked at the stick. My dad had shown me how to use a knife to take off the bark so that it would be smooth. I had a rare collection of these sticks against the back fence.

"And it's good for digging," Anibelly said. "Try it."

So I did. And so did Calvin. He digs better than anybody. He is a regular backhoe. Someday, he could become the world's best hole digger.

Dirt flew.

Water gushed.

It was great!

When our yard had more holes than the prairie dog exhibit at the zoo, we stopped.

"Anibelly, you're right," Calvin declared. "These sticks are good for digging. They're smooth in the hand, not rough."

Anibelly beamed. Calvin always has a good word for her.

"Now Alvin and I have work to do," said Calvin.

"Work?" Anibelly looked puzzled.

Calvin made a stirrup with his hands and I stuck my foot into it and he pushed me up into our apple tree. I grabbed a branch and hung from it.

"What kind of work is that?" asked Anibelly.

"It's a stretching exercise," said Calvin, "to make him taller. Being bigger will help him make friends in school."

"Oh," said Anibelly. She tilted like a teapot to look at me. "You look like a duck hanging in a Chinatown window."

"C'mon, let's help him," said Calvin. He

reached up and pulled on one foot and Anibelly copied, pulling on the other.

"See Results in Five Minutes!" said Calvin. "Amazing Results FAST!"

It hurt my armpits just a little, not too much. I could feel myself stretching like a rubber chicken.

Suddenly Anibelly let go. "Let's bake cookies with Mom!" she shrieked, and began running toward the house.

"Great idea!" said Calvin, taking off after Anibelly.

"Hey, wait!" I cried. "I want to bake too!"

Anibelly looked back but didn't stop. She was getting better at doing two things at once, like giving orders and running. "You keep stretching, Alvin," she said as she ran. "We'll bring you some cookies when they come piping hot out of the oven, okay? That way you'll be half grown by the time we get back!"

"Great idea!" I squeaked. Anibelly isn't in school yet, but she says things that sound as though she's already been through the sixth grade or something.

But it wasn't such a great idea for long. I could feel my grip slipping.

I couldn't hang on forever. I couldn't even hang on much longer!

But I couldn't jump either. I am afraid of heights. I could break some bones if I fell. So I

swung my legs up and draped my knees over the branch like on the monkey bars at school. It was a close call.

But this was not the monkey bars. I was now upside down and even farther from the ground.

And I was . . . stuck.

"Calvin!" I yelled. "Help me down!"

There was no answer for a long time. . . .

Then the scent of cookies wafted from the house.

"Hey!" I screamed. I heard milk glasses clinking, followed by the muffled voices of a TV cooking show.

Then the sound of Anibelly singing, "Lalalalalalalalalalala."

"Anibelly!" I screamed. "Help!"

"Lalalalalalalalalalala," sang Anibelly.

"Mom!" I squawked.

My breath puffed out in clouds. My face froze.

My nose ran. My
ears rang. My head spun.
Then . . . I had an itch
I couldn't reach.

But that wasn't
the worst of it.

It was getting
DARK. The wind
moved and the leaves
applauded. The garden hose hissed and slithered.
The grass disappeared, and in its place roared a
black, black sea.

"*Aaaaaaaaaaaaaaaaaaaaaaack!*" I screamed.

Somewhere a piano played.

Video games blasted.

And Anibelly sang, "Lalalalalalalalalala."

I wanted to cry. So I did. I squeezed the
branch with my knees and cried full blast. Crying is really great, even upside down. Everything
is always better afterward.

And it was. Soon I heard Louise coughing up
the driveway. Louise is my dad's wasabi-green

car, which he loves more than fireworks. My dad was home! My dad is *da dad*, which means he's the best. He would save me, he always does.

"DAD!" I yelled. "DAAAAAD! HELP ME! DAAD! I'M IN THE TREEEEE!" I screamed as loudly as I could.

There was only one problem. No sound came out of my mouth. My voice was all in my head.

Out there in the cold . . . in the dark . . . in the grasp of the evil tree, perched above the hungry sea . . . I was too scared to speak . . . and school hadn't even begun!

• • • • •

"Oh, you poor thing," said my mom, rolling me up in a blanket before carrying me into the house. "How did we forget you?"

It is easy to forget me. I don't make much noise whenever I am

scared out of my wits. And like my dad says, "Out of sight, out of mind," which means if you don't see me, you won't think of me either.

But finally, when my mom saw my empty place at the dinner table, she thought of me.

My mom is *da mom*. She never had another life, like my dad, who was probably secretly a gung fu action hero spymaster assassin before he was a dad. She was always a mom—she was practically born that way—but that's okay. She is really super-duper. She is not afraid of heights. She can climb a tree in two seconds flat and tear me—poor thing—from the grasp of the evil tree, just like that.

I love it when she calls me that: poor thing. It was almost worth hanging like a roast duck to hear it. Poor thing.

Allergic to School

"when i was your age . . . ," my dad said at breakfast the next day, "I was scared of school too. Worse, I was never a superhero before I went to school, so it was very rough."

My dad is not superhero material, but he has read practically everything ever written about superheroes and so knows us from beginning to end, which explains a lot about him.

"Just hold your head high," said my dad, "and be a gentleman."

"But I feel sick," I said.

My dad put a hand on my forehead.

"No fever," he said.

"Are you sure?" I looked at his hands. They are thick like baseball mitts. It was a wonder he could feel anything through them.

"Where does it hurt?" he asked.

"All over," I said. It was true; I was not making it up. I must have grown at least two inches from stretching so long in the tree. And growing hurts, as everyone knows.

I gave a little moan.

"Hmmm," said my dad.

I moaned a little more.

"You are not sick," said my dad.

"But I will be," I said. "I will be very, very sick. I'm allergic to school, *severely* allergic."

My dad looked at me.

"Alvin," he said firmly, putting one of his mitts on my shoulder.

"Yes, Dad."

"You will be okay, son," he said. I love it when he calls me that. Son.

I felt a little better. Maybe my dad was right, maybe I would be okay. A good word from my dad changes everything. Besides, if I missed the bus, my dad might have a few other words for me. So I dashed out of the house and caught up with Calvin just as the bus was pulling up to the end of our driveway.

"Bye, Alvin!" cried Anibelly. "Bye, Calvin!"

"Bye, Anibelly!" We waved and climbed on.

The wheels on the bus went round and round.

I was okay.

I clutched my PDK and sat next to Calvin in the back of the bus where all the fourth graders sit. The big kids screamed their heads off. I screamed my head off. We bounced up and down.

"You will be okay, son," my dad's voice echoed between my ears.

I smiled at Calvin. And Calvin smiled back.

I was okay.

Then we arrived at school.

My sneakers landed like a couple of cement blocks when I got off the bus. *Pfuump, pfuump.*

My stomach turned like a washing machine when I got inside.

I found the door that said "Second Grade, Miss Pestalozzi."

My throat tightened.

"Welcome," said a lady. "I'm Miss P."

I stopped dead in my tracks. Her hair was shiny and her skin was clean. She smelled like fresh laundry out of the dryer. She smiled at me.

But I did not smile back. I hardly even looked at her. I clutched my PDK.

I felt dizzy.

I looked around. The room was bright and neat. The walls were blank except for a picture of Henry David Thoreau and another picture of a small cabin. It is a copycat version of the original cabin that Henry had built at Walden Pond with his own hands.

"Henry David Thoreau is my hero," Esha said to her friend Flea. "You know, he kept a really cool journal. My sister says we get to read parts of it in second grade."

Everyone pushed past me. Eli shoved Scooter and Scooter shoved back. "You're it!" cried Scooter, tagging Eli, who tripped backward over Jules, who was curled on the floor waiting for Sam to leapfrog. Then Hobson and Nhia scuttled across the room like two crabs in a death lock. They were terrific!

Everything whirled around me. I was in the middle of it, but I was not in it at all.

So far, second grade wasn't any different from

first grade, which wasn't any different from kindergarten.

I was thinking about running and hiding, when . . .

"Wanna be desk buddies again?" It was Flea. She was my desk buddy in first grade. She is a girl.

I wanted to say no way. Nobody wants a girl desk buddy, except for maybe a girl. The scary thing about girls is that they are not boys. Most girls are no good at robbery and mayhem. They can't punch. But they can kick, which hurts. They skip rope too fast. They are boring. I opened my mouth to tell her all this, but . . .

My tongue turned into sandpaper.

Nothing came out.

"C'mon," said Flea, pulling out the chair next to her. "You can sit with me and Esha."

Everyone was choosing their seat and sitting down. Soon it would be too late to sit with the boys.

I opened my mouth. I wished for my voice. I wished and wished and wished. But nothing came out.

Finally, I slumped into the chair.

I was not okay.

I was so allergic to school, but I was even more allergic to girls.

CHAPTER FIVE

The Trouble with the S-Word

not being able to talk in school is a terrible problem. But having a girl desk buddy is even worse; it is the kiss of death.

At recess, I heard:

> *Alvin and Flea sitting in a tree.*
> *K-I-S-S-I-N-G*
> *First comes love.*
> *Then comes marriage.*
> *Then comes Alvin with a baby carriage!*

Oooh. It really fried my rice.

But the real problem with having a girl desk buddy is that she will follow you home no matter how hard you try to ditch her. And it is hard to ditch her when the bus stops at the end of your driveway and nearly everyone gets off and your house is right there and the whole gang can see that a girl is going up your driveway.

"Hi, Mrs. Ho!" called Flea as soon as we reached the top.

"Hello, Sophie," said my mom, smiling and using Flea's real name. "It's very nice to see you."

Mouths dropped open at the bottom of the driveway. Pinky, Jules, Sam, Nhia, Eli, Scooter and Hobson, the whole gang, stood speechless.

"It's nice to see you too," said Flea, blinking her one good eye at my mom. If there is anything good about Flea, it is this: she wears an eye patch over one eye, like a pirate. Also one of her legs is longer

than the other, like a peg leg, which is also marvelous. "I'm Alvin's desk buddy again this year."

"That's wonderful," said my mom, smiling even more and holding the door open. "Alvin is very lucky."

"Yup," said Flea. "He's very lucky."

"Would you like to come in for afternoon tea and rice crackers?"

I narrowed my eyes at Flea, which meant she had better say no and go away.

And my mom narrowed her eyes at me, which meant I had better behave like a gentleman or I had something coming.

"I'd love to!" said Flea, and she stepped right inside my house and then sat right down at my place in the kitchen across from Anibelly.

Worse, Lucy came and gave her the kiss that she usually gives to me.

"It's a terrible problem not being able to talk at school," Flea said right off. "So having the right desk buddy makes a real difference."

My mom nodded. She had that look on her face that said she thought Flea was a darling girl.

"It's a big responsibility," said Flea. "So I'm even more prepared this year than last year."

"You have a PDK?" asked Anibelly.

"No," said Flea. "But I made this." She reached into her backpack and pulled out a book. *The Book on Alvin*, it said on the cover. "I wrote the book on Alvin," said Flea.

Then Flea proudly opened her book.

Page one: " 'Alvin can talk with his eyes,' " Flea read loud and clear.

Page two: there was a drawing of two eyes, my two eyes. " 'These eyes mean he's thinking,' " I read.

Flea nodded. She turned the page.

Page three: there was a drawing of two more of my eyes. " 'These eyes mean he's okay,' " read Flea.

Page four: a pair of anxious eyes. "These eyes mean he has to go pee!" exclaimed Anibelly without reading.

"Hey!" I said.

Page five: a pair of big round eyes. " 'And these eyes mean he has bingo!' " read Flea.

"What a great book!" said my mom with that smile on her face that said she thought Flea was a very clever girl, and I had still better be a gentleman or else! "You are very observant," my mom added.

Flea beamed. "Thank you," she said. "People

think Alvin's uncommunicative, but he's really not."

"Alvin should be proud to have a friend like you," said my mom. She was so pleased that she brought out a special treat, two-thousand-year-old dragon's beard candy in a box, and offered it to Flea first.

As if that weren't enough, Flea asked for chopsticks.

Then she *sluuurp*ed her tea like she really meant it and pinched a dragon's beard candy between her chopsticks and popped it right into her mouth. She even chewed with her mouth closed the *whole* time.

"I saw dragon's beard candy on a cooking show once," said Flea, dabbing her lips with a napkin. "It's made of eight thousand strands of sugar wrapped around nuts and coconut and sesame seeds."

My mom beamed.

"I'm taking Aggression for Girls," Flea went on. "It's a combination of kickboxing and karate and it's supposed to make me stronger . . . and I

got a goldfish this summer. His name is Boatswain. He watches action movies and swims around only during commercials." She smiled and reached for another piece of dragon's beard.

I could hardly stand it.

"I think it's a stupid book," I blurted. "And you're a stupid girl."

Flea gasped. She clasped *The Book on Alvin* to her chest. Her mouth fell open, and some beard strands fell out.

"Alvin Ho!" said my mom. "You apologize right now!"

I hung my head. I had used the s-word.

I crossed my chopsticks this way.

Then I crossed my chopsticks that way.

My mom was giving me *that* look, which meant that I had better apologize or she would make dragon's beard out of me.

Yoctoseconds turned into zeptoseconds, turned into attoseconds, turned into a blink of an eye,

then into a heartbeat. Then my life crawled before my eyes.

"Sorry," I finally peeped.

Tears filled Flea's eye.

It was not a good sign. I had a terrible feeling that a gentleman would never make a girl cry, even a girl with only one eye.

Flea slipped *The Book on Alvin* into her backpack and, without a word, headed out the door.

I was so relieved and happy to see her go, I felt like dancing! If I had danced, the new look on my mom's face said, she would have broken my legs.

So I dashed out after Flea. I had a feeling that it was the gentleman thing to do, but I didn't really know, I couldn't remember.

"Hey . . . ," I huffed when I caught up with her. But Flea did not stop. She moves rather fast for someone who can see only half of everything and walks on uneven legs.

"Stop!" I said.

Flea stopped. She blinked her eye. She crossed her arms.

I breathed in. And I breathed out. I did not feel so good. I was on the sidewalk, in broad daylight—gulp—with a girl.

"Okay," I said.

"Okay, what?" said Flea.

"Okay, I'm going to mean it this time," I said.

Flea waited.

I waited.

A car rolled by.

I leaned over to see what was in the gutter.

Nothing.

Then I looked up to see if there might be any giant meteorites heading for Flea.

None.

So finally, I blurted, "I'm sorry that it's a weird book and that you're a weird girl."

POW!

I think it was an uppercut. I'd seen it on Saturday-afternoon boxing with my pohpoh. An uppercut is when you curl your arm like you're picking up a pail of rocks and you send your fist into your opponent's jaw from the bottom up. I lifted off my feet and landed on my butt. *"Owwwwwww!"* I felt like crying. So I did.

Just as I was about to duke it back to Flea, a police car rolled by. And everyone knows that a police car is much more interesting than punching a girl. It was a good thing that the police car rolled by because I come from a long line of farmer-warriors in China who have been duking it out since 714 AD and it looked like Flea had taken lessons or something and knew what she was doing, so we would have battled to the death for sure. And it is hard to say how scary that would have been.

Minutemen vs. Redcoats

if flea were a boy, everything would be different. First, she wouldn't have ignored me all morning. Second, things would have improved between us on account of boys have more respect for one another after a good pounding. But Flea is not a boy. She is a girl. And girls are weird even if they wear a cool eye patch, drag a cool peg leg and know how to throw a mean uppercut.

I was thinking about all this when . . .

"Alvin?" a voice called. "Alvin?"

My heart stopped. It was Miss P. She is very nice, but she has a habit of calling on you when you least expect it. Everyone was looking at me over the tops of their books and holding their breath. . . .

The hand on the clock clicked *tick, tick, tick.*

Someone's toe tapped *toc, toc, toc.*

My heart thumped *boom, boom, boom.*

I couldn't breathe in. I couldn't breathe out.

"Alvin," said Miss P. "Would you like to skip your turn?"

It was reading class. We were reading something about Henry David Thoreau's furniture. He had only three chairs: one for being by himself, two for a friend, and three for a party. Normally, I like reading. Like my dad, I am a great reader for my age. I can make my voice go up

Henry David Thoreau

and down and pause at all the commas and periods, just like my dad, to make everything super-duper exciting. But in school . . .

I opened my mouth. The words on the page were supposed to roll right off my tongue . . . but nothing did.

I was *not* skipping my turn, but it always *looks* like I am.

If there is anything good about reading class it is this: history class comes next.

History class is not like reading class. History is all about the American Revolutionary War, which happened back when everyone was having fights and firing cannons left and right and enjoying all sorts of explosions without getting busted.

If you live in Concord, Massachusetts, which is hard to spell, it is hard not to like history. My gunggung says it has something to do with feng shui, which is the Chinese way of saying some places are more exciting than others. The only problem with Concord is that there are no

volcanoes. If there were a volcano with explosions now and then, it would be the most exciting place in the world!

The best thing about history, as everyone knows, is that you can play it at recess.

Our favorite game is Patriots' Day, which is based on the most exciting day of the year, April 19, which is the day when the American Revolutionary War began back in 1775. Every year on that day the church bells ring like crazy, just like they rang long ago, to call the Minutemen out from their homes to fight the Redcoats. The Minutemen were the good guys. They were ready to march or fight at a minute's notice. And the Redcoats were the bad guys, sent by the King of England to capture the gunpowder and explosives that the Minutemen had hidden all over Concord.

This is how to play Patriots' Day.

First, the Redcoats march in across the playground from their hiding place behind the cafeteria.

Then the Minutemen slither across the grassy field like angry snakes from their hiding places behind trees.

They meet at the Old North Bridge, which is really the monkey bars, where the Redcoats won't let the Minutemen swing across. The Minutemen begin to swing anyway because the monkey bars belong to them, and the British say no way, they've just captured the monkey bars, so they shoot the Minutemen, who then drop dead on the wood chips.

Then the British Redcoats want to pretend to be dead too, but the Minutemen won't let them. The Redcoats pretend to be dead anyway, but the Minutemen won't stand for it so they duke it out, just like they did back in historic times. It is mayhem and chaos! It is the beginning of the American Revolution!

But before you can have a revolution, you have to choose sides.

"You guys on this side are the Minutemen,"

said Pinky, who usually does all the choosing. "And you guys on that side are the Redcoats." He pointed to everyone but me.

I wanted to play too, so I said with my eyes

that I wanted to be a Minuteman or a Redcoat, it didn't matter to me, war was war.

"Hey, how about Alvin?" asked Sam. He doesn't like leaving anyone out.

I stood up as tall as I could.

"Alvin who?" asked Pinky. He looked around. He looked up and down. Then he looked right through me. "Who's Alvin?"

Pinky is no pinky. He has been the biggest boy in my class since kindergarten because he started school late. And he's also the leader of the gang, which means if he doesn't play with me, the other boys won't either.

I wished with all my might that Pinky would let me play. But he never does. Then I wished with all my might that I could just scream! But I couldn't. I could only stamp my foot, which didn't help. I was buzzing mad like my dad's electric razor, but I couldn't buzz!

"The British are coming! The British are coming!" Pinky yelled to start the game. He was

pretending to be Samuel Prescott, the local hero who warned Concord that the enemy was approaching. It is not fair that Pinky is always Samuel Prescott, but he is the biggest boy. And the biggest boy can be whoever he wants.

"God save the king!" yelled Jules. Jules was the leader of the Redcoats.

"God save the Minutemen!" screamed Sam.

"Charge!" everyone yelled.

The gang headed for the monkey bars, where the Minutemen pounded the Redcoats and the Redcoats thumped the Minutemen until the

playground monitor came and called a time-out. It was fantastic!

Even though I wasn't a Minuteman or a Redcoat, I played dead at the end anyway because there's no law stopping anyone from lying on the soft wood chips and closing their eyes.

You can't live in Concord without loving history, but I sure wished that I loved recess too.

The Best Way to Avoid School

the best way to avoid school, as everyone knows, is to get sick.

But not all sicknesses are created equal. Some are better than others.

Tonsillitis, for example, is pretty good. You get all the Italian ice you want. It is my dream to have tonsillitis someday.

Appendicitis is good too, but not as good as a *burst* appendix, which gets you a ride in a wailing ambulance speeding through all the red lights on Route 62 to Emerson Hospital. This happened

when Calvin's appendix burst and our mom found him on the kitchen floor. He has all the luck!

The flu is okay, but it's not great. You only get ginger ale and crackers, which is a real rip-off, but usually you get to watch all the cooking shows and cartoons you want.

The common cold? One bad-tasting zinc drop, some tissues and you're back in school the next day.

Medical mysteries? If you get foreign-accent syndrome or barking madness or squeaky chalk phobia, forget it. You're back in school the *same* day.

So you have to be patient. It's like choosing a car, or a house; my mom says you shouldn't jump at the first offer because a better deal might be right around the corner.

And it was.

One day, Jules was out—with chicken pox.

"Don't go near Jules's house," Miss P warned our class. "It'll take two weeks for all the blisters

to scab over completely. Until then, Jules is highly contagious."

Highly contagious?

I felt like dancing!

I nearly burst like fireworks!

But I didn't.

I had to wait until after school.

•••••

It was hard *not* to go near Jules's house. It is on the way to everything. It is as though Jules's house is a big magnet and I am an iron filing, and every time I so much as step out of my house, I am yanked toward it, just like that.

When I finished after-school tea with my mom and finally stepped out of my house, that was exactly what happened! I was sucked by such a powerful force toward Jules's house that I could barely even pick up the fat frog in the gutter on my way. And when I got to Jules's house, there was already a line behind

the tall bushes in front, just like the line at the cinema when there's a scary movie playing.

"Hey, guys," I said.

"Shhhhhhhh," hissed Eli. "Stay low or Jules's mom will see us and we'll all get sent home."

"Wait your turn or shove off," said Hobson, who always gives you a choice. "This is a top-secret under-cover operation. We go in one at a time, or we don't go in at all."

"Okay," I said. "I'll wait."

"*Urrrrrgh,*" said the frog in my hands.

"What's that you got? A frog?" asked Nhia.

"Yup," I said.

I set the frog in the grass and everyone leaped around trying to catch it for a while. It was fabulous! Then before I knew it, it was my turn. I caught my frog, rushed around the side of the

house and ran right into Pinky under Jules's window.

"Watch where you're going," said Pinky. He held out a can. On the can was a label:

One-minute visit: 50¢

Jump into bed: $1

"You got a dollar?" Pinky asked.

I gasped. Normally, Pinky does not speak to me. Usually I do not show up on his radar, not one bleep, not even a flicker.

But I was flickering now!

I shook my head. I did not have a dollar.

"You got fifty cents?"

"No."

"I'll take that frog, then," said Pinky.

"No way," I said, tucking the frog into my armpit. "It's for Jules."

"No dollar, no frog, no service," said Pinky.

"Wait," I said, remembering an unchewed piece of gum in my back pocket. I took it out. It was warm and soft.

Pinky grabbed the gum, unwrapped it and stuffed it into his cheek. "Okay," he said, gnawing. "You get a minute."

I took my frog and hopped through Jules's window.

Jules was in bed.

I gave my frog to Jules.

"Thanks," said Jules.

"*Urggggh-rrrrgh,*" said the frog. "*Urrrrggggh.*"

"So where's the chicken?" I asked, glancing around Jules's room.

"I was wondering that myself," said Jules. "I wish I knew."

I was really disappointed. How do you catch chicken pox without first catching a chicken?

"I came to catch the *chicken* pox," I said. "Not the plain pox."

But the plain pox wasn't too shabby. It had turned Jules's head into a potato covered with red eyes. Some eyes were crying, others were crusty like sugar on a cookie. It was great! Jules had never looked scarier!

"So whatcha doin'?" I asked.

"Nothing," said Jules. "Well, maybe I'm scratching a little."

Jules was scratching like crazy. I do not know if Jules is a girl or a boy. Sometimes Jules plays with the boys, and other times Jules plays with the girls. "Jules" could stand for "Julian" or it could stand for "Julia." It is hard to tell. The blisters didn't help either. In fact, they made Jules look like neither boy nor girl. Instead, Jules looked a good deal like an alien. A real live alien potato fresh off a UFO.

"You're so lucky!" I said. "I'd love to look like that."

"Yeah," said Jules. "It's really great except for the itching."

"You got any you can't reach?" I asked.

"Yeah, right up the middle of my back," said Jules, squirming.

So I gave Jules a hand. I think it is one of the

rules of being a gentleman, but I don't really know, I can't remember.

"Thanks," said Jules.

"Anytime," I said.

"Time's up!" Pinky hissed from the window.

"Dude," I said.

"Dude," said Jules.

•–•–•

None of us caught a chicken or even saw one. So none of us broke out with the chicken pox that day. Or the plain pox either. It was a terrible disappointment.

Then a long time later . . . just when we'd forgotten all about Jules and the chicken pox, and none of us were trying to catch anything anymore . . . a miracle happened.

Our art teacher, Mr. Gruenert, was showing us famous self-portraits one warm afternoon.

Frida Kahlo looked a little itchy to me with branches coming out of her hair.

Paul Gauguin looked a bit feverish because he was in Tahiti, where it's really hot.

And Vincent van Gogh, in his scratchy straw hat, *definitely* looked itchy.

Very itchy.

Then we got mirrors and brushes so that we could paint our own self-portraits. My self-portrait was going to be a masterpiece, but strangely . . . I didn't feel like painting. I didn't feel like doing anything at all.

"You boys look a little strange," said Mr. Gruenert.

I felt strange.

Then I looked into the mirror. Something scary stared back.

"Aaaaaaaaaaaaaaaaaaaaaaaaack!" screamed the whole gang. They were looking in their mirrors too!

Then Flea, who was next to me, looked at me. *"Aaaaaaaaaaaaieeeeeeeeeee!"* she shrieked, spilling her paints.

The other girls screamed too. Some ran fast. Others ran faster.

You'd think we were a bunch of aliens or something.

School shut down for two weeks and a half after that. There was a story about us in the newspaper so that people as far away as Andover, Massachusetts, which is also hard to spell, read about the great chicken pox epidemic in Concord. We were famous! The newspaper said . . .

The first victim had been carefully quarantined.

All the children had been warned to keep away.

How the epidemic ever got started was a complete mystery.

Johnny Astro

having school shut down was really fabulous.

Even if it meant scratching like crazy.

I wore my Firecracker Man outfit all day.

I didn't have to carry my PDK.

I didn't have to worry about being a gentleman.

Best of all, I didn't have to sit next to a girl, except for Anibelly, who doesn't count on account of she's my sister and there's just no avoiding that.

Somehow Calvin and Anibelly also got the chicken pox and together we watched all the cooking shows we wanted.

Our mom made us Italian ices.

Our pohpoh rubbed us with lotion.

Our gunggung told us stories about when he was little and had the chicken pox in China. His family had chickens. He chased the chickens. The chickens chased him. Then he got the pox. He was so lucky!

We chilled out completely.

Even my dad stayed home a couple of days to chill so that my mom could go to work. And whenever he chills, he reaches for his favorite toy—Johnny Astro.

It is a special occasion whenever my dad plays with his Johnny Astro. It means he is in a really good mood. And playing with the toy puts him in an out-of-this-galaxy mood. Best of all, it means that I get my dad all to myself. Calvin and Anibelly always sneak away whenever Johnny Astro comes out. We've watched Johnny Astro all our lives, and now neither one of them enjoys watching it anymore. But I do.

"When I was your age . . . ," my dad began. He always begins with a story about being my age whenever he reaches for his Johnny Astro. "There was nothing I loved more than Johnny Astro. Not my ant farm, not my walkie-talkie, not my power drill, not even . . . my baseball card collection."

I love stories about when my dad was a kid. Sometimes they are funny, like how it used to snow so much they had to dig tunnels through the snow for air, and sometimes they aren't funny, like when his yehyeh died and everyone was so sad they forgot to feed YehYeh's bird, so his bird died too.

"When I was your age," my dad continued, "Johnny Astro made me very popular. Everyone wanted to play with me because I had a Johnny Astro."

"Everyone?"

"Absolutely," said my dad. "No one ever saw a toy like this. No one."

I read the box. "Johnny Astro," it said. "Really Flies. No Wires. No Connections. FLY YOUR SPACE CRAFT ANYWHERE."

"If you can fly one of these," my dad said breathlessly, "you can fly anything."

He put batteries into the plastic control panel and flipped the switch. A fan whirred softly and he moved the stick shift like a pilot.

Suddenly a balloon with an astronaut launched into the air! The balloon swirled and hovered silently above our heads as if by magic.

I blinked rapidly. I breathed rapidly. Fireworks burst inside my eyes.

"You can take off . . . you can land it . . . fire the propulsion, knock it down, capture it, fly it again," said my dad. "To the moon—at full throttle!"

The balloon went up, up, up, and landed on a high shelf. Then it floated off the shelf as if lifted by an invisible hand.

"Can I try?" I asked. I had watched my dad play a million times, but I had never played with

it, not even once. But I had the pox . . . and who could say no to a poor thing with pox?

"Only . . . if you're careful," said my dad. "It takes a special touch."

"Cross my heart," I said.

I commandeered Johnny Astro up and over our heads and then smoothly onto a landing pad on the coffee table.

My dad was very impressed. "Amazing!" he said, blinking rapidly. "You're as astonishing as I was at your age! You're top gun."

He shook his head.

He wiped his eyes.

He put his hand on my back.

"Someday," my dad said in a low whisper, "this will be yours."

I gasped. I didn't know what to say. My dad had *never* said that before. And my dad *always* means what he says. I think it is one of the rules of being a gentleman, but I don't really know, I can't remember.

I only wished that Calvin and Anibelly had

been there to hear it too, in case my ears were playing tricks on me, which they sometimes do.

"M-m-mine?" I could hardly say it.

My dad nodded. "Sure, son," he said.

•-•-•-•

That night I had a dream that I was Johnny Astro himself! I got into Johnny Astro's balloon and blasted straight into orbit. I went over the tops of everything, even the moon! I sailed across the inky sky. It was thrilling! Everything was great . . .

Until I looked down.

Then nothing was great. I felt dizzy. Our driveway pinwheeled under my sneakers.

Then I crash-landed and woke up.

I ran downstairs.

I looked up.

And there, in the moonlight, on the top shelf of the highest bookcase, was Johnny Astro, safe and sound.

TGID. Thank God it was only a dream.

A Real Nightmare

my dad is really good at taking care of his things. Maybe it is one of the rules of being a gentleman, but I don't really know, I can't remember. "Take care of your things," my dad likes to say, "and your things will take care of you."

He takes such good care of his car, Louise, for example, that she will probably run for a third geological age, although

she already has one transmission in the junkyard, which, my mom says, is the car equivalent of having one foot in the grave.

My dad also takes good care of our house and our yard. He can use a hammer. He can climb a ladder. He can climb down too, usually. And he owns a power drill in a box.

He takes really good care of his children too. Just look at us—a couple of weeks of scratching ourselves to death and we were practically normal again, on our way back to school.

So when my dad wasn't playing with his Johnny Astro, he kept it in its box and set the box on the top shelf of the highest bookcase for safekeeping.

The Johnny Astro sure was amazing, even sitting in its box. I headed into the living room to look at it one last time before going to school. "Johnny Astro made me very popular," my dad's voice replayed itself in my ears. "Everyone wanted to play with me. . . ."

"Johnny Astro," I read across the box for the

millionth time. "Really Flies. No Wires. No Connections. FLY YOUR SPACE CRAFT ANYWHERE."

I stared, unblinking.

I shifted my PDK under my arm.

I swallowed.

"Alvin," my mom yelled from the kitchen. "Hurry, honey, your bus is almost here!"

"Coming, Mom!" I yelled back.

But first . . . all I needed was a stool and to str—eeeee—eeetch until I could reach it. Johnny Astro was perfect for show-and-tell.

"Someday," my dad's low whisper filled my ears, "this will be yours."

Someday. I had no idea that someday would be today!

"Thanks, Dad," I whispered. "You're the best." I even remembered my manners.

Then I slid the box into a large shopping bag . . . and I slipped out the door.

"What's that?" Pinky asked as soon as I got on the bus.

I gasped. I could hardly believe it. I was already flickering on Pinky's radar!

"Johnny Astro," I said.

"What's Johnny Astro?"

"The greatest toy ever made," I said.

"Never heard of it," said Pinky. "What does it do?"

"I'll show you at show-and-tell," I said.

"But you don't do show-and-tell," said Hobson.

"I do too," I protested.

"You show, but you never tell," said Sam.

Sam was right, I never tell. But I was fabulous at show. I knew how to pick 'em. If something tells a story, and as long as I can reach it and it is something I can carry without using a wheelbarrow, it is probably perfect. I've brought in all sorts of treasures . . . my dad's

fantastic reading glasses . . . my mom's pearl necklace that she looks so good in . . . Calvin's baseball card collection.

And now Johnny Astro.

"If this is the greatest toy ever made, you should show-and-tell *now*," said Pinky, "*before* we get to school, or we'll never know what you wanted to say."

It made perfect sense. I could hardly wait anyway. I pulled the box out of the bag.

The gang read the box.

All jaws dropped open.

All tongues fell out.

"That's just the box," I said. "Wait till you see it in action!" I fingered the edge of the cover.

"Open it," Sam pleaded. "Open it."

I held my breath.

I wanted to open it. I wanted to show the gang the most fabulous toy ever made. I couldn't wait.

Whoosh. I lifted the cover. An old smell of fun and excitement filled our noses.

Then *whoosh*. The bus rounded a corner.

And we rounded in our seats.

And when we all sat back up . . . Johnny Astro didn't look the same. There were a few pieces . . . missing.

They were not in the box.

They were not in the bag.

Or in the aisle.

Or under the seats.

They were *nowhere* to be seen.

I was not even sure which pieces were missing. But there were a few empty spaces in the plastic package where there should have been parts.

"OH NO!" I cried. "MY DAD'S GOING TO KILL ME!"

The noise on the bus went round and round. It was so loud that my voice got lost. No one turned around. Even the driver's eyes, which usually lift into her mirror whenever there is an extraordinary outburst, did not shift.

I swallowed. I blinked. I did my best not to cry. The wheels on the bus went round and round. I bounced up and down. But then a tear rolled down my cheek. Then another. And another. Before I knew it, I was crying full blast. Crying is really great. Everything is better afterward . . .

Except when the next stop is school.

And when you walk into class, you find a substitute teacher.

"Alvin Ho," called the sub. She was taking attendance, which is where most of my troubles usually begin with subs.

I opened my PDK. I needed an escape route.

"Alvin," the sub called again.

"Here," answered Flea.

"You are Alvin Ho?" asked the sub.

"No, ma'am, I'm Flea," said Flea. "That's Alvin." She pointed at me.

The sub looked at Flea and then at me, over the top of her glasses. "He can answer for himself," she said.

"No he can't," said Flea.

"Why not?"

"He just can't," said Flea. "He's Alvin Ho."

The sub's eyebrows arched like two unconnected bridges. "I will have no funny business in my classroom today, is that clear?" said the sub.

Flea nodded. Then her lips curled in, which meant that she had more to say. "Alvin talks normally at home," Flea continued, "but at school he only talks with his eyes."

"Oh?"

"Just watch his eyes," said Flea.

I rolled my eyes, not on purpose, they just rolled on their own like a couple of loose pearls from my mom's necklace the time I borrowed it for show-and-tell.

"Oops," said Flea.

"Is this a joke?" asked the sub.

"No, ma'am." Flea shook her head.

The sub looked puzzled. "No one mentioned a special-needs student. . . ."

"Alvin's not special," Flea explained matter-of-factly. "He just doesn't speak in school."

The sub fixed her gaze on Flea. Then she locked her gaze on me. It meant that I needed to be on my best behavior.

Fortunately, I've had lots of practice in good behavior. I knew what to do. I kept my eyes low. I kept my hands in plain sight. I stayed in my seat.

Then show-and-tell began.

Jules showed a pox scab.

"Ah, that's nothing," said Eli. So then Eli showed his. It was redder than Jules's.

But it wasn't redder than Hobson's, which was *crimson*.

But that was nothing compared to Esha's, which was practically still oozing.

Then everyone began raising their shirts and lowering their pants to see who had the biggest and ugliest scab of all. It was fabulous!

Then the substitute said that that was enough of the scabs. But some of us had taken off so much of our clothing by then that it took a while to get it all back on.

Then the dreaded moment came.

"Alvin," said the sub. "Do you have a show-and-tell?"

I froze. I avoided eye contact.

I held my breath. I sucked in my gut. I clutched my PDK.

"His show-and-tell met with some misfortune on the bus this morning," said Flea helpfully. "So it can't be shown."

"Misfortune?" said the sub. She gave me the

stare that said I wasn't yet finished with misfortune.

So, slowly, I pulled out the box.

"Johnny Astro!" gasped the sub. "I had
one of these. It's the best toy in the
world! It really flies! You can fire it up,
send it into orbit and bring it down
again. It is absolutely spectacular!"

The class went silent. No one
moved. No one even breathed.

The sub got very quiet. She wiped
her eyes. "Nothing else like it was ever made,"
she sighed.

Then she smiled at me.

And I smiled back just a little. Maybe it is
even a gentleman's rule to smile back when a
lady smiles at you, but I don't really know, I can't
remember.

For a sub, I guess she was okay.

As for show-and-tell, it was the best thing I
had ever brought in. Everyone wanted to play
with me at recess.

"We'll get it up in the air in no time," said

Pinky, carrying the box out to the playground. "I'll hold it while you fix it."

I nodded.

Then we lifted off the cover. The missing pieces were back! But they were wrecked.

"I found them in the back of the bus," said Flea. "And put them back in there for you."

"Don't worry," said Eli, whose father fixes cars. "I can fix anything. My dad showed me how."

"I can do origami," said Sam. "I'll make you a new balloon!"

"Here are some Band-Aids," said Eli, peeling a dirty one from each elbow.

"And I've got spray paint at home if you want to come over after school," said Nhia.

I opened my PDK. There were instructions for surviving practically every disaster except a Johnny Astro disastro. That's the problem with PDKs, you never know what you're missing until you are missing it.

"Alvin," said Flea, putting a hand on my shoulder. "People will think you were careless, but you really weren't."

"It was an accident," said Nhia.

"Yeah, an accident," echoed Eli. "It's a good thing that it wasn't your dad's."

My heart sank like a dead battery.

And I don't think I really need to tell you what happened next.

CHAPTER TEN
Facing the Music

my dad is not only a gentleman, but he is *da man*, which is a lot like being *da dad*, which means he can handle quite a lot.

He can eat wasabi without crying.

He can watch a scary movie without flinching.

He can carry a big heavy rock straight across the yard and set it right where my mom wants it.

And he can carry it back again if my mom changes her mind.

When he's had a bad day, my dad can play the piano like crazy until he is his old self again . . . or if he's had a truly horrible day, he can curse a wild blue streak like William Shakespeare.

"Sorrow on thee, thou spongy onion-eyed hugger-mugger!" my dad might say. Then he'd write it down. Or "Clean thine ears, thou lumpish bum-bailey!" Every time he thinks of a new curse, he writes it on a little piece of paper and puts it in a tin. Cursing like Shakespeare always makes him feel better.

That's my dad. He's *da man*. He can handle just about anything.

So right after school, I put Johnny Astro back where it belonged.

And I slipped in between Calvin and Anibelly, where I belonged, and we waited with Lucy by the window for our dad to come home.

"Are you *sure* Dad said it was yours?" asked Calvin.

"Maybe we should just have your funeral now," Anibelly whispered sadly.

But I was in luck. When our dad finally stepped through the door, he was in an unusually cheerful mood.

"Hi, everyone!" he said cheerfully.

Silence.

"What's up?"

Silence.

"How 'bout some more fun with Johnny Astro today?"

No one said anything. My dad whistled across the living room. Cheerfully, he reached for Johnny Astro.

Cheerfully, Johnny Astro came down. "Really Flies," said the box. ". . . FLY YOUR SPACE CRAFT ANYWHERE."

Then my dad opened the box.

His whistling stopped.

His breathing stopped.

His feet stopped.

Then he staggered backward.

"WHAAAAAAAAAAT IS THIS?" he wailed. "Johnny Astro, what happened to you?" he cried.

Then he really cried. He put his head in his
hands, and his shoulders went up and down.

Carefully, I put my arm around my dad. Crying is really great. Everything is better afterward. Usually. But this was not usual. This was the best toy ever made.

"WHAT BOOTLESS TOAD-SPOTTED BLADDER DID THIS?" my dad howled. "I'LL SEE THEE HANG'D!"

Gulp.

"WHAT HAPPENED TO MY JOHNNY ASTRO?" he screeched.

And my mom rushed in to see what was going on.

"ALVIN?" my dad bellowed.

My chin quivered. My face wrinkled.

"Dear, you know Alvin can't speak when he's frightened," my mom said calmly.

"This isn't about speaking," my dad said. His teeth were clenched. "It's about respecting other people's things!"

I wanted to cry. But I couldn't. I had to save it for when things got really rough, which I could see was coming faster than a meteorite falling from the sky and aiming straight for me.

"Maybe it was an accident," squeaked Anibelly.

"An ACCIDENT?" howled my dad. "How can an accident happen on the TOP shelf?"

"Maybe he needed a good show-and-tell," said Calvin. "And the accident happened on the bus."

"WHAAAAAAAT?" roared my dad.

It was time. I began to cry. Crying is really great, it is a good way of softening the blow coming to you. And it helps if the tears run off your chin and you slobber a little and your eyes get puffy and you are a real mess.

"Oh, Alvin, you poor thing," said my mom, which really helps too. She put her arms around

me. If lightning struck, it would hit her first, which is probably one of the rules of being a mom.

"This is more than an accident," said my dad. He held up the newly repaired and heavily bandaged Johnny Astro.

"Maybe the guys tried to fix it at recess," said Calvin.

My dad turned seaweed green.

Then he turned sea-foamy.

Then he turned pomegranate, then grapefruit, then orange. Normally I like orange. It is the color of tigers and sherbet and sunsets and mango. But I did not like this orange. It was danger-alert orange, which is only helpful around construction sites.

Anibelly and Calvin stared with their mouths wide open. Getting busted is the best spectator sport around our house, except when you're the one getting busted.

"My Johnny Astro . . . ," my dad wailed. He put the cover back on it and hugged the box sadly. Then he marched off to the piano, like he

always does when he's had a hard day, and played like a wild savage beast.

My dad learned to play the piano when he was about my age. So now when he plays, he sounds like Brahms even though his fingers are as thick as bratwurst. As long as he was playing I was okay. And the longer he played, the more okay I was going to be, because as we all know, music is medicine. The more you take, the better you feel.

Finally he stopped. "Alvin needs piano

lessons," said my dad. "It will keep him busy. It will give him confidence. It will change his life."

My dad paused. "It might even give him a good show-and-tell," he added.

And so it was decided that I would take piano lessons, which was really marvelous! I was expecting a grounding, but instead, I was going to face the music.

"Thanks, Dad!" I cried.

My dad said nothing.

I wanted to say something else, something that would make my dad feel good for taking it easy on me. But I didn't know what else to say . . . until I thought of something.

"Someday when I'm old and beastly and have sausages for fingers, I will play the piano just like you, Dad, instead of punishing my kid for destroying my Johnny Astro."

Hair grew on the backs of my dad's hands. He looked strangely beastly again. I think he needed more music to smooth his soul.

The Whole Tooth

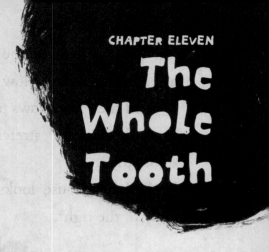

piano lessons were a splendid idea except that every Wednesday after school, when I could have been doing something really useful like taking a bath or vacuuming my room or sharing my sticks and toys with Anibelly, I was to go to Miss Emily's house—alone, without Lucy, without Anibelly, and worst of all, without my Firecracker Man gear or PDK. I might as well have been completely naked!

Now, Miss Emily was no ordinary piano

teacher. She lived at the very end of the street where the trees hang low.

And the grass grows tall.

And shadows stretch like inky tentacles across the road.

And her house looks like a face that sags sadly to the right.

"Go straight to Miss Emily's," my mom said. "She's expecting you. Don't stop anywhere."

I might not have had a problem going to Miss Emily's—that is, if we lived in a normal town. But we do not. A lot of famous dead

people live here. And when you are famous, you don't get buried like a regular person under a stone that has your name and telephone number on it. You have to stay in your house to give tours.

The way to know where a famous dead person lives is to look for a sign on their front lawn that says it is their house. For example, at the other end of our street, away from the end where Miss Emily lives, there is a big white house with a sign that says "The House of Ralph Waldo Emerson." Mr. Emerson was famous for writing essays, which is to say he got famous for doing a lot of English homework.

Mr. Emerson died a long time ago, but he still lives in that house. On Thursdays he sweeps his walk. It is very creepy. But his is not the only house like that. There's the "Orchard House, Home of the Alcotts," where Louisa May Alcott leads tours and shows where she used to write stories at a small desk. I've taken the tour with my family. She is definitely a dead author still in her house.

"Calm down," my mom said when we were in Orchard House. "She's an actress dressed up as the author."

I don't think so. It wasn't a show at all. It was for *real*. You could just tell that she had always lived in that house. And her next-door neighbor, Nathaniel Hawthorne, who was also famous for writing stories, is another dead author still in his house. He has a sign outside that says "Wayside." We didn't make it over there after touring Orchard House that day on account of I was scared so stiff I had to be carried home.

So in a normal town I would not have a problem going to Miss Emily's. But this town is not normal.

And Miss Emily's house is not normal. There is a sign on her front lawn. So halfway there, I stopped dead in my tracks. I couldn't bear to get any closer.

"Boo!" said a voice.

"*AAAAAAAAAIEEEEEEEEEE!*" I screamed.

It was Jules. It is hard to go anywhere without

going past Jules's house, as I've mentioned. And Jules was in the bushes out front.

"You going to piano lessons?" asked Jules.

"Maybe."

"Looks like you were headed straight to piano lessons."

"Maybe I am and maybe I'm not," I said.

"No one walks this way except to go to piano lessons," said Jules. "I see 'em coming and I see 'em going. Mostly they come. Only the lucky few ever go."

"What do you mean?"

"I don't really know," said Jules. "There are only rumors."

"What rumors?"

Jules looked down the street both ways, then whispered, "You know the witch with the yummy house who fattened the kids?"

I nodded. I sure hated that witch who fed Hansel and Gretel to fatten them and then tried

to shove them into the oven. She was the most evil witch in the world, worse even than the one who gave Snow White the poisoned apple, on account of she had kept Hansel and Gretel in a cage, which, as everyone knows, could mean years of therapy for them.

"Just learn your scales," Jules said. "But don't eat anything if she tries to feed you. You don't like brownies, do you?"

Gulp. Brownies are my weakness.

"Brownies are her specialty," Jules continued. "You're not going to last very long if you like brownies."

I gasped. Then I turned and dashed home.

When I arrived in my yard, I was in luck. Anibelly was digging with my sticks and Lucy was doing yoga ball next to her. Lucy puts a ball on top of her front paws, stretches out in the down-dog position and touches the tip of her nose to the ball. She can hold the pose until the

squirrels come home, or until Anibelly is finished digging holes.

"Anibelly," I shouted. "Come with
me, and bring Lucy
too."

"Okay," said
Anibelly. "C'mon,
Luce." Anibelly is
fantastic. She always comes when I ask and she
never questions why until she has figured it all
out, which usually takes a while.

"Aren't you supposed to be going to piano
lessons?" she asked when we reached Jules's
house. Jules was no longer in the bushes.

"I heard there were going to be snacks," I said.
"Just thought you might want to come along."

Anibelly stopped. She put her hands on her
hips. She put her left foot out like in the
Hokey Pokey, which is her favorite dance.
Then she looked at me sideways. "Is that the
tooth, Alvin Ho, the whole tooth and nothing but the tooth, so you can help God?" she
asked.

Anibelly tapped her toe and waited for an answer.

"Okay . . . I'm allergic," I finally coughed.

"Allergic to piano lessons?"

"No. Allergic to the piano teacher."

"Why?" asked Anibelly, puzzled. "Does she have three fingers?"

"Three fingers???!!!!" A piano teacher with three fingers is like an airplane with only one wing! "I thought she was just the witch from 'Hansel and Gretel'!" I cried.

Anibelly gasped. She hated that witch as much as I did.

"What are you going to do?" Anibelly wanted to know.

"There's only one thing *to* do!" I said. "Capture her and tie her up!"

"Hooray!" cried Anibelly. She sprang up and down. Then she did her Hokey Pokey foot again, which was not a good sign. "Then what?" she asked.

"Then we'll . . . we'll . . . we'll figure something out," I said.

Anibelly shook her head. "Take me home, Alvin Ho," she said. "Take me home right now."

"But I need you," I pleaded. "You're good with strangers. They're always nice to you. And they're nicer to me when you're with me."

"You might be Hansel, but I'm no Gretel," said Anibelly. "I'm Anibelly Ho and I dig holes. I don't sit in cages."

Then Anibelly clung to the bushes in front of Jules's house like a tick to flesh. I could not pry her free until I had promised to take her home. So I did. I took her home. Maybe it was the gentleman thing to do, but I don't know. I didn't care. She really was no use anyway, all balled up like that.

"Don't worry," said Anibelly when she was safely back in our yard and had unballed herself. "Just hold your head high and be a gentleman."

A gentleman? I needed to be Firecracker Man! But it was too late. I would never find all the pieces of my costume in time. I was already

late. And late is not good if you're a gentleman, I think.

So I turned and headed back toward the witch's creepy old house.

Just as I was passing Jules's house again, something strange ambled out of Miss Emily's house and started coming toward me.

I froze.

It got closer and closer. . . .

My mouth opened, but nothing came out.

"Mr. Ho?" the figure called. "Are you little Master Ho?"

I did not nod. I did not shake. I did not even breathe. I was not Mr. Ho. I was Alvin Ho. Mr. Ho was my dad. And who was *Master* Ho?

"Heavens, child, you look like you've seen a ghost," said the old woman who stopped in front of me. "We all know there are plenty of 'em around here!" she cackled. It was only a little cackle, but it was a cackle, just the same. "I'm Miss Emily. Your mother called and said you were on your way. We were both worried that you had not yet arrived."

She was just as I had imagined. She was about three hundred years old and a half. She bent like a question mark toward the sidewalk and she looked exactly like her pictures in *The Complete Brothers Grimm Fairy Tales, Deluxe Edition*. There was no doubt that this was the very same witch who had fattened Hansel and Gretel and tried to feed them into the fire. She was the most evil witch in the world, and even worse now for being disguised as a piano teacher.

"Come along, sweetie," she said.

Sweetie? I put my foot down, just like Anibelly, in the Hokey Pokey way. I was going nowhere.

But then I caught a whiff of my pohpoh's almond-scented hand lotion, which is very pleasant. Miss Emily smelled exactly like my pohpoh! Strangely, my feet began to move . . . and before I knew it . . . I was following her like her own shadow! If only Anibelly were with me! She would have helped me resist following my nose, which I have no control over.

Soon I was at the place where the trees hang low.

And the grass grows tall.

And shadows spill like ink across the road.

We floated past the sign in Miss Emily's yard that I couldn't read because we were moving too fast. Then we went right into the mouth of the house that sags sadly to the right.

Inside, it was a dark and stormy night.

A painting of a young woman sitting at a piano stared straight at me.

An enormous white head of Beethoven with blank eyes scowled angrily from a corner.

A plate of brownies sat obediently on the coffee table, a glass of milk beside it.

My eyes moved from the painting to Beethoven to the brownies. Then they stayed on the brownies, which were perfectly dusted with the kind of sugar that looks like fresh-fallen snow. My mouth watered.

"Would you like a snack before we begin?" Miss Emily read my mind. "I made my special

brownies. Quadruple fudge . . . they're still warm

from the oven."

Oven?

Gulp.

"Just learn your scales," Jules's voice echoed inside my ears. "But don't eat anything."

I stepped back. Then I tripped and fell over the piano bench.

"Oh dear," cackled Miss Emily. It was only a little cackle, but it was a witchy kind of cackle just the same.

I was speechless. I didn't know what to say. If I had known that taking my dad's Johnny Astro would end me up in such trouble, I *never* would have taken it.

"Let me help you up," said Miss Emily. Her bony hand and crooked fingers stretched toward me . . . closer . . . and closer . . . until . . . I could see—she only had three fingers!

I can't tell you what my lesson was like after that on account of there was no lesson.

I was completely frozen, like a piece of sausage off a truck.

PSYCHOtherapy

no one can explain why I can't talk in school and now at piano lessons, so once a month, after school, my mom drives me to see a children's psychotherapist to get to the bottom of it.

A therapist is a very smart person who wears glasses and can help you with your problems by asking a lot of questions instead of giving you shots, which is really amazing. But a psycho, as everyone knows, is a crazy person in the movies that you never want to run into in real life. So a

*psycho*therapist is a very smart crazy person that you should stay away from for your own good.

I tried to explain this to my mother, but I can never get the words out on account of it's hard to talk about scary things. So I have to outsmart the psycho on my own. It's not easy, but I had it figured out.

ALViN HO'S PSYCHO SURVIVAL RULES

1. Carry your PDK.

2. Never volunteer any information.

3. Never look her in the eye.

4. But keep an eye on her.

5. Expect the unexpected.

6. Escape at the first chance.

7. Have a Plan B.

So when my mom dropped me off, I was ready.

"Did you have a good day in school today?" the psycho asked.

I avoided all eye contact.

"Do anything special?"

I kept my hands in plain sight.

"Working on your pitching?"

I nodded. I am always pitching and catching with my gunggung.

"That's good," said the psycho. "I bet you're terrific."

I nodded again.

"How are the piano lessons going?"

Silence.

"Read any good books lately?"

I nodded. I had read a bunch of great books with my dad. We love true tales of courage and accounts of dangerous expeditions. *Tenzing Norgay and the Sherpas of Everest* was especially exciting.

"How's Lucy?"

It was a trick question. There is always so much to tell about my dog. But I caught myself. I've never said a word in therapy. It is too scary. What do you say to a *psycho*?

The clock on the wall clicked *tick, tick, tick*.

Outside, cars swooshed by in the rain.

The psycho sighed.

She shuffled some papers.

"Want to play cards?" she finally asked.

Usually, playing cards is okay. When she runs out of questions, the cards come out and it means the therapy part is over, and when it's over, it's over, and it is just me and the psycho . . . alone . . . with nothing to do . . . but play cards . . . and wait for my mom or dad to pick me up . . . *tick, tick, tick*.

Psychos sure can shuffle. *Flip, flip, flip.*

But she doesn't play very well. She talks too much.

"Making friends is tough, isn't it?" she jabbered.

I held my cards.

"Making friends is hard for grown-ups too," she went on. "So I know how you feel."

I did not move.

"Do you sometimes want to play with kids who don't want to play with you?" she asked.

I nodded. Then I won the first hand.

Shuffle, shuffle. Deal, deal.

"We can't make people play with us who don't want to," said the psycho.

Then I won the second hand. It was too easy. She wasn't paying any attention to her cards.

Then I won the third hand. "But there's always someone great to play with," the psycho jabbered on, "who is also looking for a friend."

The longer we played, the more I won . . . and the more she lost. But she didn't just *lose*, she hardly even looked at her cards! If I played like that, Calvin would have a few unsavory names for me.

"Wipe thy ugly face, thou weedy earth-vexing whey-face," Calvin would say. "Methinks you stink, thou pribbling beetle-headed harpy."

The psycho stopped. "What?" she said. "What did you say?"

Oops. Did I say something?

I kept my eyes low. I kept my hands in plain sight.

"I had no idea you knew Shakespeare." She sounded surprised.

I was surprised too. I didn't know Shakespeare. Shakespeare lived a long time ago. Now he's dead. How could she think I knew him?

"Why, that's really wonderful!" she continued.

But it wasn't wonderful. I hadn't meant to say anything at all. It had just sort of *slipped*.

"I don't know Shakespeare very well," the psycho went on, "but I'm *thrilled* that you can express yourself in that way."

"Sit thee on a spit," I muttered, "then eat my sneakers, thou droning beef-witted nut hook."

Oops. I couldn't stop myself! That's the problem with cursing. Once you start, it's hard to stop.

"Grow unsightly warts, thou half-faced horn-beast!"

"Bathe thyself, thou reeky reeling-ripe pigeon egg!"

The psycho gasped. The look on her face said she didn't think it was so wonderful anymore.

So I made a break for it.

I bolted from my poker hand and ran as fast as I could.

Unfortunately, the psycho was even faster.

She nabbed me as I got to the stairs.

So I let her have it.

"Away, I say, thou currish milk-livered mold-warp!

"Get thee gone, thou beshibbering onion-eyed flap-dragon!

"THY MOTHER WEARS ARMOR!"

Rule No. 2

my dad arrived just in the nick of time. If he had been a minute later, I would have gone to Plan B, and who knows how scary that might have been!

My dad did not scream.

He did not yell.

He did not turn eggplant or edamame or Chinese radish or danger-alert orange.

He was not pleased with the psychotherapist's report, but he did not bust me either.

Louise headed for home, making all right-

hand turns because she cannot turn left anymore. She has AA, Automotive Arthritis, she is that old.

And I knew I was headed for trouble. I was thinking of getting a head start on all the crying and wailing I needed to do to soften the blow coming to me, when Louise made a couple of unexpected right turns and before I knew it, she had pulled right in front of Brigham's Ice Cream!

"Did you take a wrong turn?" I squeaked from the backseat. Usually we go to Brigham's to celebrate a birthday or a good report card, but never before for cursing a grown-up.

"No, son," my dad said. I love it when he calls me that. I like it even more than my own name, which I like a lot.

"Then why are we here?" I asked.

"Therapy is rough, right?"

I nodded.

"I had a rough day too," said my dad.

I held my breath.

"So we need to stick together," my dad went on, "and we need some ice cream."

"Oh?" I said. The last time I didn't get the punishment coming to me, I ended up with something worse . . . *way* worse.

"You mean I'm not getting busted?" I asked.

"No, son," said my dad. Normally, I love it when he calls me that. But this was not normal.

Inside, my dad and I walked past other children eating ice cream with their parents. We scooted into a booth.

Tears streamed down my cheeks.

"*Waaaaaaaaaaaaaaaaaaaaaaaaaaaaaaaaaaah!*" I wailed, just in case. Our waitress stepped back.

Then I wailed some more. After that I felt much better.

The Triple Monkey Triple Fudge with whipped cream and cherries on top helped too.

But my dad was the most helpful of all.

We had a heart-to-heart, man-to-man talk, just between me and my dad. And this is what I discovered . . .

1. My dad tries to be kind to everyone.
2. He loves superheroes.
3. But he wouldn't rather be one.
4. He'd rather be my dad than anything else in the whole universe.

5. If he could change anything about himself, it might be his bald spot, maybe.
6. If he could change anything about me, it would be nothing.
7. He didn't have a friend until he traded someone a Carl Yastrzemski Rookie for a Hank Aaron Rookie.
8. After that they were best friends.
9. His wish for me is to find a good friend.
10. His second wish for me is that I'd enjoy Shakespearean curses only for fun, not for insulting someone.

"Son," said my dad. "I know it's frustrating and change comes very slowly, but you're making good progress in your therapy."

Then my dad explained that while Rule No. 1 of being a gentleman is no hitting, Rule No. 2 is no cursing or insulting.

"Not at all?" I asked.

"Not one word," he said. Then my dad stood up and puffed out his chest. He looked ten feet tall. My dad is amazing.

I stood up. I puffed out my chest. I did not look ten feet tall. I didn't even look half that size. But it was okay.

"Ready, son?" he said.

"Ready, Dad."

Then I put my arm around him and we went home.

It was the best time I ever had with my dad.

CHAPTER FOURTEEN
The Apes of Math

i was making great progress. I could finally remember some things about being a gentleman:

HOW TO BE a GENTLEMAN
1. No hitting.
2. No insulting.
3. No making anyone cry, even if she is a girl who has only one eye.
4. Apologize if you break RULE No. 3.
5. Don't duke it back (see RULE No. 1).
6. Lend a scratching hand to someone with pox.
7. Take CARE of your things.

I could hardly believe it! Suddenly I was closer to being a gentleman! But I was not any closer to having friends.

Fortunately, I remembered that I had some good advice about that from Calvin. It was right there in my PDK:

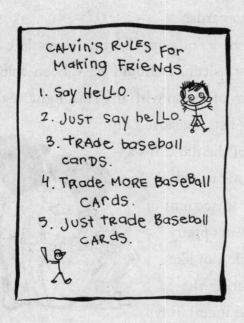

CALVIN'S RULES for
MAKING FRIENDS

1. Say HeLLO.
2. JUST say heLLO.
3. TRAde baseball caRDS.
4. TRAde MORE BaseBall CARds.
5. JUST TRAde Baseball CARds.

The list was useless . . . until I crossed off:
1. Say hello.
2. Just say hello.

Now it was perfect! And since the advice had come from Calvin, I was sure that he meant *his* baseball cards, on account of I didn't have any. And because he didn't write his name on his baseball cards, it could only mean one thing . . . but I asked anyway.

"Calvin," I said, "could I borrow a couple of your *best* cards?"

Srrrrr, srrrr, said Calvin. It was late and he was fast asleep. I should have been asleep too, but I am often up with my flashlight, reading or making lists, because I am afraid of the dark. It's a great time to talk to Calvin on account of he is always pretty agreeable, not like he is during the day, and it certainly sounded like Calvin said "Sure, sure."

•●•●•

The next day, I gave the Hank Aaron Rookie to Pinky.

He said nothing.

Then I gave him the Carl Yastrzemski Rookie.

He said nothing.

Then I had nothing else to give.

"Man," Pinky finally said. He stuffed the trading cards into his back pocket and walked away.

Then slowly, my life began to change . . . at recess, Pinky kicked the soccer ball past where I was standing. It was fantastic!

Then during library time, Pinky grabbed Sam's book, so Sam grabbed it back. Then Pinky took it again, so Sam kicked him, which made Nhia jump on Pinky. All this happened right in front of me, between the shelves on earthquakes and volcanoes and the shelves on bats and whales. If I had poked out my arm I could have gotten it broken

in several places, which is practically an invitation to jump right in, which I would have done if the librarian hadn't leaped first.

Then in math class, we got a worksheet on the cost of Henry David Thoreau's house:

How much did Henry's house cost?	
Boards	$ 8.03 +
Used shingles	4.00
Laths	1.25
Two second-hand windows	2.43
One thousand old bricks	4.00
Two casks of lime.	2.40
Hair	0.31
Mantle-tree iron.	0.15
Nails	3.90
Hinges and screws	0.14
Latch	0.10
Chalk	0.01
Transportation.	1.40
TOTAL	$ 28.12 +

Math is okay. I don't have to read anything out loud. No one holds their breath to see if I am going to take my turn or pass.

The first question asked "What material cost Henry the least?" That was easy.

Next, "How many bricks did Henry buy?" That was easy too.

"Pssssst," hissed Pinky. "What's the answer?" I was on his radar again! I could hardly believe it! My dad and Calvin were right. Baseball cards really do work!

Pinky leaned over and copied my answers onto his paper. Not only was I on Pinky's radar,

but all my answers were on his paper too! Then he motioned for Eli to copy his paper. Then Scooter leaned over and copied from Eli.

"*Ahem,*" said Flea. Flea has only one eye, which is okay, but unfortunately, that eye sees everything, which is annoying. "Cheaters are losers," she said disapprovingly.

"Cyclops are losers," Pinky hissed back.

Flea gasped.

"Fauntleroy," said Miss P. That's Pinky's real name, Fauntleroy, but no one ever calls him that except for grown-ups. "Would you please come up to the board and answer the first question?"

Pinky went up and wrote his answer, *my* answer.

"That's very good, Fauntleroy," said Miss P. "You're getting quicker and better at math."

Pinky beamed. Then he sat down.

Flea gave him The Eye.

Then Eli took his turn. And Miss P said he did a fine job.

But when he got back to his seat, he got The Eye too.

Next Scooter got his turn. And Miss P said he was great. Normally, he is not great in math, numbers are a mystery to him. He got The Eye.

Then before I knew it, math class was over.

In fact, school was over.

And I never got my turn! Only the apes of math got turns. It was not fair! I was as mad as a salmon swimming upstream.

And so was Flea. Her eye was big and round. "It's really not fair you didn't get your turn," said Flea as we were leaving.

I nodded.

"After all, they were all *your* answers," she added, just as we passed Miss P standing in the doorway saying good-bye to everyone. I was really glad that Flea let Miss P know.

Then we got on the bus.

"Hey, buddy," Pinky said when I sat down.

Buddy? He was calling me buddy?

"You're okay," said Pinky, sitting down next to me. "But you gotta get rid of that girlfriend of yours." He laughed and pointed at Flea, who had sat down in the seat in front of me.

I shrank. I knew that Flea took no nonsense. But Pinky didn't know. He was *this* close to taking an uppercut from her.

"Maybe you could play with us sometime," said Pinky.

"Really?" I could hardly wait.

The wheels on the bus went round and round. We bounced up and down.

"But . . . you'll have to do a few things first," said Pinky.

"Like what?" I asked.

"I'll let you know," said Pinky.

"Does everyone have to do them?" I asked.

"Just you," said Pinky. "It's a new rule, dude."

I swallowed.

"Okay." I swallowed. "Dude."

The Problem With Joining a Gang

the first problem with joining a gang is that the pressure starts right away.

"I dare you to stick your tongue out at the bus driver," ordered Pinky. The gang followed us off the bus.

I stood in my driveway. I stuck out my tongue at the bus driver. She didn't look too pleased. But Pinky did.

"I dare you to yell a bad word at the bus," ordered Pinky as the bus pulled away. "Now!"

"ZOUNDS!" I yelled at the top of my lungs.

"What?" asked Eli.

"Behold thy mirror, thou spleeny, knotty-pated dewberry!" I added, for good measure.

"Okay, forget it," said Pinky impatiently. "Whatever."

The second problem with joining a gang is that Flea gave me The Eye, then turned and went down the street, swinging her cool peg leg and all, without a word.

The third problem with joining a gang is that you don't know what they'll make you do . . . but I had a feeling it would be scary. I thought about this as we walked up my driveway.

"I dare you . . . ," said Pinky, looking up, ". . . to jump off the roof of your house!"

"I'm telling Mom," said Calvin, who was right behind us. He ran into the house. "Mo-o-o-om!" I heard him yell. "Mo-o-o-o-om!"

My heart thumped like crazy. My mom is an ace rescuer. She would save me. She always does.

But my mom did not come out. And neither did Calvin.

So I scratched the old pox on my left side. Then I scratched the old pox on my right side. Then I looked up at the roof of my house. It was a long way up. I swallowed. It was all I could do not to cry. But it is important at moments like this to not show how you really feel. It is like playing poker. Even if you're losing, you have to pretend you're winning.

"Well?" said Pinky.

"Okay," I said. But I was not okay. I could just about pee in my pants! One moment I am standing in my driveway, the next moment I could be *on* my driveway, *dead*, just like that.

"Well?" said Pinky. "What are you waiting for?"

"I gotta use the bathroom first," I said. I ran inside, rushed up the stairs and used the bathroom.

Then I went into my bedroom and looked out the window.

It was a long way down.

Calvin and Anibelly were playing catch with GungGung in the backyard. Farther down the road, Flea was playing by herself in her own backyard, building something that looked like a pyramid. It was fabulous, even from far away.

"This is a fastball." GungGung's voice floated up into my ears. He is my grandpa from my mom's side. When he is at my house after school, it means that my mom is at work and he is here to keep his eye on things.

I looked down at Pinky. He was shouting something at me and his face was very pink. He looked *much* smaller than he used to. In fact, from where I was, Pinky was just a pinky!

I went back downstairs.

"I'm not going to jump off my roof," I told Pinky.

"Why not?"

"I have acrophobia," I said.

"Huh?" said Pinky.

"Fear of heights," I explained.

"Well, then . . . ," said Pinky. "I dare you . . . to . . . watch a scary movie!"

I froze. I hate scary movies. They give me nightmares. After I watch one, I can't eat, I can't talk, I can't walk, I can't sleep, I can't get it out of my head. But I supposed it was better than jumping to my death in my own driveway and then having Louise run over my dead body.

I wanted to cry like the end of a rain pipe on a rainy day. But I didn't. It is important at moments like this to not show how you really feel. It is like marching to the doctor's office for a vaccination. Even though the shot could kill you, you still have to look like you don't know it.

So I began to march.

Fortunately, the longest path to the TV at our house is through the backyard.

"Hi, Alvin!" called Anibelly cheerfully. She is always happy to see me, especially after school. "Was that you cursing like an infectious, pox-marked measle at the school bus?"

I didn't answer. Anibelly was wearing *my* mitt, the one with *my* name on it. And she was throwing *my* ball, the one that used to belong to Daisuke Matsuzaka, with her two fingers together on top. She snapped the ball into GungGung's glove. *Ffffppht*. It was a fastball, all right, but it really wasn't that fast. She was just *pretending* it was fast.

But the *sound* of Anibelly's fastball smacking into the mitt is a little scary. It stopped the gang dead in their tracks.

"You want to throw, Alvin?" asked Anibelly. "I'll catch."

"No thanks," I lied. "I've got something better to do."

"Like what?"

"Like prove his bravery," said Pinky, "so that he can play with us at school."

Anibelly narrowed her eyes. She put out her Hokey Pokey foot and made a face that said they were going to have to deal with her first.

"Anibelly," said GungGung. "If Alvin would rather not play catch, it's okay."

My gunggung loves baseball. He is an ace pitching machine. And playing catch with him is our favorite thing to do after school whenever he is around. So Anibelly and GungGung went back to throwing the ball and the gang and I stood there and watched.

"This is a knuckleball," GungGung said, showing Anibelly and Calvin. He bent his two fingers at the knuckles so that they came up like two rabbit ears on the ball, and pitched it to Calvin. *Ffffslurrruuullluuurpf.* It was slow and tricky. Calvin hardly knew where it was going!

"This is a changeup," said my gunggung. He shifted his middle finger and fourth finger to grip the ball from the top, with the index finger

and pinky gripping from the sides and the thumb on the bottom, and snapped it into Ani-belly's glove. *Ummmmph*. It looked like a fastball

but was a bit slower. Another tricky ball. It can fool you into swinging early.

Then my gunggung demonstrated the two-seam fastball and the four-seam fastball. Then the split-finger and its cousin, the nastier, slower forkball. They are *baaaad*, meaning they are fantastic!

I could hardly stand it. I love throwing with my gunggung. I love it more than digging holes. And I definitely love it more than doing dares from Pinky. To make matters worse, there was Anibelly using my glove and ball!

"I thought you boys had something better to do," said GungGung.

No one moved. A breeze swirled crispy leaves up and around our ankles.

"Oh yeah . . . ," said Pinky finally. "We do."

And that is the worst problem with joining a gang. Someone else speaks for you.

A Horrific Thing

by the time we came up from the basement after watching *Alien Babies Land from Outer Space*, it was getting dark. The house was very quiet except for the wind weeping and wailing through the walls and the faint machine-gun sound of my mom's sewing machine coming from upstairs. Besides being an ace pitching machine my gunggung also likes to sew.

"That w-w-wasn't a very s-s-scary movie at all," stammered Scooter.

"N-no, it wasn't," said Eli.

"I've s-seen s-s-scarier," said Nhia, shuddering.

I said nothing.

"Let's go throw some b-balls," said Pinky.

"Okay," said Hobson.

"*Woohoo!*" said Pinky, picking up my ball and glove, which Anibelly had left by the door. "We even have an autographed b-b-baseball by Alvin Ho!"

The gang slapped high fives.

I slapped nothing.

"I think there's s-s-something wrong with Alvin," said Sam.

I could hardly move. I could hardly blink. I could hardly breathe. I could hardly do anything but watch alien babies invade Earth and crawl around like zombies, over and over again in my mind.

But Pinky and the gang had already gone out, and so had my glove and ball. And so I followed, like a zombie myself.

Outside, it was a dark and shadowy night.

The tree reached its crooked fingers toward me. The garden hose slithered and hissed.

Usually, no one pitches at our house when it gets dark. You can't see what you're doing and if you miss, you could have a terrible accident.

"I'd like to learn the forkball," Pinky said to me. "Show me." He threw me the ball and backed up.

I froze. A forkball is a killer. It is slow and nasty. Even in daylight, you can hardly tell where it's going. If Pinky didn't catch it, the ball could smack him right between the eyes.

"C'mon!" said Pinky. "You waitin' for retire-ment or something?"

I shivered. I squinted. It was hard to tell the gang apart from the other creepy shadows in the yard.

"I haven't got all night!" screeched Pinky.

So I wound my pitch, leaned back on one leg, then fired it with all my might. . . .

There was no thud in the glove.

A thick, soupy silence poured into our ears.

Then *CRAAAAAAACK!* The sound of a window splintering into a million diamonds.

Oops.

"I think I hear my mom call-ing," said Pinky. He tossed my glove and had started across the yard when . . .

A Horrific Thing emerged from the shadows . . . and came charging toward us. Half of it was green and the other half was black. Scales ran along one side, and warts ran down the other.

I was ready to pee in my pants. But I didn't. At moments like this, it is important to have already used the bathroom, which I had.

"*AAAAAAAAAAAAACK!*" Pinky screamed a belly-button-piercing scream. "*AAAAAAAAAA-AAAAAAAAAAAAAAAAAAAAAAAAAACK!*"

The wind howled and hammered at the house. The fence groaned and creaked.

I wanted to scream my head off, but I couldn't. Nothing came out.

My heart stopped.

My breath stopped.

My eyes shut. When I opened them again, I saw that Pinky had—peed in his pants!

I didn't know what to say. And neither did the rest of the gang. What do you say when someone's just embarrassed himself to death?

The Horrific Thing moved closer. "Lalala-lalalalalala," it sang.

Pinky turned and ran. "*AAAAAAAAAAAA-AAAAACK!*" he screamed.

"Hi, Alvin!" said the Horrific Thing. It was Anibelly's voice . . . but it was not Anibelly. "Lalalalalalalala," it sang again.

Had the Horrific Thing swallowed Anibelly?

"Do you like my Halloween costume, Alvin?" said Anibelly's voice. "GungGung just finished it!"

The Horrific Thing twirled menacingly one way and then menacingly the other way. It was uglier than any of the alien babies and scarier than the whole movie from beginning to end.

"Wh-wh-what are you?" I asked.

"Half witch and half dragon," said Anibelly's voice. "I couldn't decide, so GungGung said I could be both!"

"Oh," I said.

Then—surprise, surprise—I remembered to say something nice to Anibelly. "You look terrific!" I said, even though she was ugly enough to make you run.

"You'd better come in now," called my gung-gung from the house. He was a dark shape against the bright light in the doorway. Anibelly and I ran toward the light.

"Lucky your mother wasn't home," my gung-gung said as I stepped past him. "You can tell her what happened in the morning."

I nodded. Then I looked over my shoulder. The rest of the gang had disappeared. Our yard was quiet. The house next door was completely dark and quiet too.

Lucky the neighbors weren't home either.

Death by Volcano

after breakfast the next morning, and after I had forgotten to tell my mom about what had happened with the gang, I dashed over to Pinky's house as quickly as I could. Pinky was still in his pajamas watching cartoons. I was in my Firecracker Man outfit from head to toe. It was Saturday. The world needed saving and there was no time to waste. But first . . . I tapped on his living room window.

"I want a refund," I said when Pinky came to the door.

"What refund?" asked Pinky.

"The Hank Aaron Rookie and the Carl Yastrzemski Rookie," I said. "I want them back."

"But I thought we were friends," said Pinky.

I had thought about it all night, in between reruns of alien babies crawling around inside my head. And this is what I thought: playing with Pinky was not a good trade for the cards.

"I don't like doing the things you do," I said.

"Why not?" asked Pinky.

"I'm just not talented in that way," I said.

Pinky shrugged. "Yeah, you're right," he said. Then he went back into his house. When he came to the door again, he handed over the cards.

The Rookies were okay. There is a good reason why baseball cards are in plastic pockets. It

keeps them dry, in case of accidents. I breathed a sigh of relief.

"You sure you want to do this?" Pinky asked.

I nodded. I was very sure.

"If I don't play with you, who will?"

I shrugged. I didn't really know. But I knew I didn't want to play with him.

.•..•.

Flea's house was on the way home. It is not on the way to everywhere, like Jules's house, but it is on the way to some things, some of the time.

And Flea was in her yard, swinging her arms wildly and kicking her peg leg and her regular leg equally wildly. "Ha!" she screamed, chopping her arms through the air. "Ha-ha!" She chopped the other way.

"Hi," I said.

"Ha!" said Flea, kicking the air behind her.

"Whatcha doing?"

"Aggression for Girls," said Flea. "Want to try? It's fun!"

I shrugged. "Okay." I squeezed through a loose board in the fence.

Flea sliced her arm like a sword through the air. She added a kick to the side. It was fabulous! I sliced and kicked too. "Ha!" she screamed again. "Ha-ha!" "Ha!" I copied. "Ha-ha!" We chopped and kicked until we were out of chops and kicks. After that we went inside and watched an action movie with Boatswain. He swam around like crazy during commercials, but he stayed fixed in one spot in his bowl during the action scenes, unblinking, watching the movie. It was the most amazing thing I had ever seen.

"I'll trade you a Carl Yastrzemski Rookie and

a Joe DiMaggio Rookie for your fish," I said, holding out the cards.

"No way!" said Flea.

"How about the rookies *and* . . . a piece of gum!" I said. I reached into my back pocket, but the gum was not there. Then I remembered that I had traded it to Pinky long ago.

"This fish is not for sale," said Flea. "He's family. Isn't that right, Boatswain?"

Boatswain nodded, I swear it. "Why, how now, putz . . . ," I began in a Shakespearean curse. Then I stopped myself. I cleared my throat.

"I have something to say," I said.

"Okay," said Flea.

I looked around. I didn't really want to say it. It was something hard to say. It was much harder than cursing or insulting.

"Can I try on your eye patch?" I asked.

"Okay," said Flea. She pulled it off and I pulled it on.

I blinked. It was fantastic!

Flea's good eye blinked too. Her other eye looked as soft as a baby's and stayed shut.

"You're blind in that eye?" I asked.

"Yup," said Flea.

"How come?" I asked.

"I come from a long line of pirates," said Flea.

It was just as I'd thought. "Is that how you got a peg leg too?" I asked.

"Yup," said Flea.

I nodded, speechless. Then I gave Flea her eye patch back.

"Was that what you wanted to say?" asked Flea.

I shook my head. It wasn't at all what I had wanted to say. But now I had run out of other things to say. So I had to say it.

"I'msorrythatIdidn'tstickupforyouyesterday-inmathclassandonthebus," I said.

Flea blinked.

Then she blinked again.

I held my breath.

"Okay," she finally said. "I forgive you."

What a relief.

So then I asked the question I'd been dying to ask, "What's that in your backyard?"

"C'mon," she said. "I'll show you." We hurried outside.

And there, in Flea's backyard, in broad daylight—gulp—was a real live VOLCANO! It was HUGE. It was made of mud and dirt and something called chicken wire, but there were no chickens, only wire.

Flea poured a bucket of vinegar and some baking soda into the top and lava bubbled out. It was a MESS! And it was AMAZING!

After the bubbling stopped, it got kind of quiet in the backyard.

Flea looked at me.

And I looked at Flea.

"What are you going to be for Halloween?" I finally asked.

"A princess," said Flea. "I'm always a princess."

"Oh," I said. I didn't like princesses. They are stu . . . I mean silly. Princesses make me sick. And just as I was about to say

how much I hate princesses, I heard something else come out of my mouth.

"You'd make a good princess."

Grow unsightly warts! How did I say that?

"Thank you," said Flea. "What are you going to be?"

"A gentleman," I said.

"Oh," said Flea.

It grew kind of quiet again.

Then she remembered her manners.

"You'd make a good one," she said.

"Thanks," I said.

Then we poured more vinegar and baking soda into the volcano. Lava bubbled out like crazy.

"Death by volcano!" I screamed, leaping and jumping over the foamy lava.

"*Rrrrrrrrrrrrrrrrrrrrrrrrrrrrrrrrrrrr!*" roared Flea, leaping and jumping like crazy too. There were plastic Minutemen and Redcoats and trucks and motorcycles and packs of ferocious tuojiango-saurus and a flock of velociraptors that we had to

save. So we did. It took all afternoon, but we saved them all.

After we finished, Flea brought out her book, *The Book on Alvin*. She drew Firecracker Man saving the world from death and destruction on the side of a volcano. It was really super-duper!

"Do you think we can do this again some-time?" I asked.

"Sure," said Flea. "Anytime."

Anytime. It sounded like something friends say to each other.

And I blasted off toward home.

•●•●•

"Alvin," said my mother when Firecracker Man blasted into the kitchen.

Uh-oh. The look on her face was not so great.

"Did you put a baseball through the neighbor's window?"

"What baseball?" I asked innocently. "Not I."

"It was in her sink," said my dad. "And it had your name on it, son."

I love it when he calls me that, usually.

Alvin Ho's
Woeful Glossary

Alvin Ho—(1) Aka Firecracker Man, (2) a gentleman-in-training.

American Revolutionary War—Started in Concord, Massachusetts, which is hard to spell. Revolutionaries fired cannons and all sorts of gunshots at the British to get rid of them. It took a long time, from 1775 to 1783, with lots of help from France, Spain and the Netherlands. But in the end, the British went home and the American colonies became a new country.

Anibelly—(1) Messes with my things, (2) eats my food, (3) drinks my chocolate milk, (4) generally gets in my way.

Beethoven—(1) Aka Ludwig van Beethoven, (2) famous German composer, (3) wrote nine symphonies, one violin concerto and lots of hard stuff for the piano, (4) scary-looking.

Boatswain—Pronounced "BO-sun." (1) An officer on a ship in charge of the maintenance of the vessel, (2) the name of Flea's fish.

Brahms—(1) Aka Johannes Brahms, (2) another famous German composer, (3) born six years after Beethoven's death, (4) loved Beethoven's music, (5) kept a marble bust of Beethoven that looked down on him while he composed.

bratwurst—German sausage.

Calvin—(1) Knows everything, (2) owns everything, (3) is quite agreeable late at night.

Carl Yastrzemski—Pronounced "Ya-STREM-ski." Nicknamed Yaz or Captain Carl. Played his amazing entire twenty-three-year career with the Boston Red Sox. He was a left fielder, a first baseman and a star hitter. He is the Red Sox all-time leader in career RBIs, runs, hits, singles, doubles, total bases and games played and is second for home runs, behind Ted Williams. His dad was a potato farmer.

chicken pox—It's just itchy pox. A chicken doesn't come with it.

Chinese radish—A vegetable that looks like a big white carrot.

Concord, Massachusetts—(1) Birthplace of the American Revolution, (2) eighteen miles northwest of Boston, (3) home of famous dead authors (see below), (4) my home, (5) hard to spell.

Daisuke Matsuzaka—Born in Japan in 1980 and nicknamed the Monster in Japan and Dice-K in the United States. K means strikeout! During his first season with the Boston Red Sox in 2007, Dice-K broke the Red Sox rookie record for the most strikeouts in a season, with 156. He finished the season with 201 strikeouts and became the first Japanese pitcher in history to start and win a World Series game.

edamame—Pronounced "ed-a-MA-may." A vegetable that looks like peas in a pod.

feng shui—Pronounced "fung SHWAY." A Chinese way of placing stuff, like houses and

furniture and trees and rocks, so that everything looks fantastic!

Flea—(1) A girl, (2) short for Sophie, (3) her grandpa, who couldn't hear very well, thought her parents had said that her name was Flea when she was born.

flybox—(1) Also called a tackle box, in which different flies, plugs, spinners, jigs, spoons, poppers, lures, hooks, lines, bobbers and sinkers are stored for use in fishing, (2) handy for holding a PDK.

Frida Kahlo—Mexico's most famous woman artist. When she was six she had a disease called polio. Her right leg became very thin and the kids at school called her Frida *pato a palo,* or Frida "peg leg."

gung fu—Aka kung fu or gong fu. Chinese exercises that look cool in the movies, but that break things around the house when you go crazy practicing them after watching a gung fu movie.

GungGung—(1) Ace pitching machine, (2) ace costume maker, (3) my mom's dad.

Hank Aaron—(1) Aka Hammer, Hammerin' Hank or Bad Henry, (2) set the Major Baseball League's home run record of 755 in 1976, (3) a 1952 Topps Hank Aaron Rookie card sold for $100,000 in 2000.

Henry David Thoreau—Pronounced "THOR-ow." Famous dead author who loved nature. Built a small cabin in the woods and lived in it for two years before he got tired of it and moved home.

Johnny Astro—A toy that really flies. Invented in the 1960s by toy genius Sol Friedman. Hard to find. Impossible to repair. If you break it, you might as well plan your funeral.

kickboxing—Not real boxing. Involves punching the air while bouncing back and forth in a boxing dance. Usually done in a class at the Y.

kimchi—Pickled cabbage that explodes in your throat and makes you cry.

Louisa May Alcott—Famous dead author who wrote *Little Women*. Wrote at a small desk

her father made for her. Lived in the brown house on Lexington Road. Still does.

Minutemen—A small handpicked elite force of the Massachusetts militia, who were "ready in a minute." They were the first to arrive at a battle during the American Revolutionary War.

Nathaniel Hawthorne—Famous dead author who wrote *The Scarlet Letter* and *The House of the Seven Gables* and many short stories. Loved taking walks with his wife, Sophia. Lived next door to Louisa May Alcott. Still does.

Patriots' Day—A holiday commemorating the Battles of Lexington and Concord, the first battles of the American Revolutionary War, fought on April 19, 1775.

Paul Gauguin—Pronounced "goh-GAN." French painter who lived in Peru with his mom for four years from the time he was about Anibelly's age to the time that he was my age. Then he moved back to France. When he was older, he lived in Tahiti and painted the people there, using bright colors. A friend of Vincent van Gogh.

PohPoh—(1) My grandmother on my mother's side, (2) good at rubbing stuff on chicken pox, mosquito bites, bee stings and scraped knees, (3) keeps an eye on GungGung.

psychotherapy—A scary way to help you not be so scared.

Ralph Waldo Emerson—Famous dead author who wrote many essays. Took long walks with his friend Henry David Thoreau. President Abraham Lincoln came to dinner at his home once. Lived in the big white house on Cambridge Turnpike. Still does.

Redcoats—Soldiers of the British Army during the American Revolutionary War. Red was the color of their uniform.

Tenzing Norgay—The first to climb to the top of Mount Everest with Edmund Hillary in May 1953.

tourniquet—A tight band tied around a limb to stop severe bleeding. Used to find a vein for blood donation. Also used in the event of amputation.

Vincent van Gogh—Dutch artist who flunked out of many different jobs before he discovered that he was a painter at age twenty-seven. He liked painting peasants and poor people. When Vincent painted at night, he stuck candles in his hat so that he could see better.

Walden Pond—(1) Looks like a big lake to me, (2) just right for swimming, (3) in the old days, they used to harvest ice here in winter and pack it in hay and put it on a train that took it as far as Chicago, (4) Henry David Thoreau built his cabin here.

wasabi—Pronounced "wa-SAH-be." A green paste made from horseradish that you eat with sushi. Explodes inside your nose and makes you cry.

William Shakespeare—Dead English author. Born after Christopher Columbus discovered the Americas, but died before the British Army wore red. Wrote lots of plays, poems, curses, everything. When he ran out of words, he made up new ones. Never lived in Concord.

yehyeh—Chinese word for grandpop on your father's side.